MURDER BEACH

EVELYN WOLPH KRUGER

Maple Creek Media
Hampstead ◊ Maryland ◊ United States

Printed in the United States of America

ISBN-13: 9780991244218
ISBN-10: 0991244214

MAPLE CREEK MEDIA

P.O. Box 624
Hampstead, MD 21074
Toll-Free Phone: 1-877-866-8820
Toll-Free Fax: 1-877-778-3756
Email: info@maplecreekmedia.com
Website: www.maplecreekmedia.com

To all the wonderful teachers and practitioners of writing at University of Iowa Summer Workshops, in the Romance Writers of America, and the Space Coast Writers Guild. Many, many thanks to each and every one of you. To those who read and critiqued this particular manuscript—thanks for your encouragement and apt corrections.

PROLOGUE

"Wanda, I don't know what I'm going to do. Look at this bill. It's worse than we thought." Mazie jabbed her forefinger on the assessment she'd found tacked to her door. "Where in the world am I getting sixty thousand dollars?" Her neighbor set a mug of coffee and some doughnut holes on the glass-topped kitchen table. Not for the first time, she had the feeling Wanda was too big for the room.

Small as Mazie was, the two of them created a crowd; she felt like she'd been crammed into a Jack-in-the-box. No, Jill in the box. She shuddered.

"You don't have to pay it all at once," Wanda said. "The condo association will let you spread payments over a three year period."

"Even twenty thousand tops my Social Security checks for the entire year." Mazie wiped moisture from her eyes with the back of a trembling hand.

"Can't that kid of yours up in Maine pay the bill? He's a banker, for God's sake. Besides, he'll sell the condo when you die and get his money back."

"He's tapped out with the twins in college and running for tax collector. I told him to stay out of politics, but will he listen to his dear old mama?" Mazie sipped from the mug. "Absolutely not! Anyway, I already asked him."

"What did he say?"

"Wants me to sell the unit and to move up to Sheldon Center. He thinks I could buy an apartment across the road from the beach and take care of the younger kids so he and that woman he married can travel. I say if he wants a second family, he should take care of them. I'd be nothing but a frost-bitten babysitter. No thanks!"

"It's not cold all year round in Maine. Some people love the summers along the coast."

"When it's not cold out the mosquitoes get you. What do you think brought me to Florida in the first place? How are you paying your assessment?"

"Look around, Mazie. This condo is half the size of yours and has only one balcony. I took out a reverse mortgage at the bank. No monthly payments."

"Yeah, but the loan company gets your property when you die. I want to leave something to my grandkids."

"That's pure foolishness. Let them work for their own money the way we did."

"Easy for you to say; you still have a job. If I'd worked longer my pension would be larger. Actually, when I married Ed Nashun, he had plenty. That damn Sun Cruise outfit got most of our savings. Ed was no fool, but he did love the craps tables."

"They've cut me back to part time at the hospital, but you really are in a deeper hole. I won't let you starve; have another doughnut." Wanda refilled the plate and added steaming coffee to Mazie's cup.

"What do you think of Quick and Easy Cash? Byron said he'd treat me right."

"That's like incest. He manages the condos, collects the assessments, and then makes high-interest loans to tenants. His deal stinks like rotten carp."

"What else can I do? I'm too old to get a job and I'll starve to death before I ask my son for money again."

Wanda stood, came around the table, and circled her generous arms around a sobbing Mazie.

"There, there, honey. Wanda won't let her friends suffer. I'll take care of you."

CHAPTER 1

Saturday night, July 5th

David Paul Santorino stopped thirty feet from the dark green dumpster and held his breath. A raccoon scaled the vertical side of the over-filled bin and crept inside. In the glare of halogen lamps, its tiny claws and teeth shone as the animal tore into a plastic bag. A photo op if he ever saw one. He put down his two sacks of groceries and backed quietly toward his rented Buick.

This would be the first picture in his vacation album—a thief caught red-handed by an FBI agent in Sunny Shores, Florida.

The camera's flash startled the furry creature and it fled—but not before David noticed what lay beneath its claws. Vacant eyes stared at him from a rip in the black plastic. He removed his shoes, moved closer, checked the woman's carotid artery, and took additional pictures. He stepped carefully so his footprints wouldn't contaminate the scene.

A few minutes later he stood in the kitchen of the ocean-side unit his sister Martha had rented and called the police about the body.

"I'll be down as soon as I put my groceries in the refrigerator." He gave his name, the condo number, the phone number, and his badge number. His entire life had come down to a bunch of impersonal digits. Even the letters in his name were just zeros and ones as far as the computer at the station house was concerned.

He unpacked jars of baby food and zwieback for Susan; animal crackers, Cheerios, and Fruit Loops for Andrew; Brie, grapes, and Cabernet Sauvignon for Martha; steaks, Edy's coffee ice cream, and bourbon for himself. He'd thrown in some fresh vegetables to keep his sister happy. Publix had been a zoo. He knew better than to shop for groceries on a Saturday evening in a resort community, but he'd had her list. Martha's flight arrives in Orlando tomorrow noon, and he'd be ready. With her husband, Lucas, busy keeping peace in Iraq, she'd been glad for the chance to relax with him on a beach.

It had been a lonely year since Mia moved out of the house they'd occupied for ten years. Was she happier now? He stuffed down the uncharitable hope that she was not. He shouldn't care about her any more than about that emaciated body in the dumpster. Both were souls beyond his reach, but fortunately Martha and her children were not.

He hadn't gotten used to being alone. He still reached for Mia in the middle of the night and by morning found himself hugging the pillow on her side of the bed. The final divorce decree rested on the top of his dresser back in Kansas City, and she now lay in someone else's bed. He tried to shake off the agonizing image of his wife wrapped in the pale hairy arms of the Walgreen pharmacist, a man who never stepped outside in daylight hours.

Yes, he'd gone to inspect the rival, knowing it made him a despicable sneak. His wife's lover had stood behind the pharmacy enclosure pecking intently at the computer keys, his myopic eyes fixed on the monitor. No horse play, no jokes with the techies. How could his wife have rejected him for such a boring nerd?

Correction. His former wife.

~~~~~~~~~~~

Martha promised him she'd bring a sack of paperback books about fictional crimes. Nothing real, nothing probable, just outrageous, imaginative, and evil. Now he'd stumbled on the real thing. Bad beginning! He felt every pain too damn much. He even felt a stab of sorrow for the pitiful old woman in the dumpster. Why wasn't he cool and independent like a steely-eyed mystery detective?

Back downstairs, he found three police cars. A rumbling fire truck filled the exit to the street, and a rescue vehicle throbbed near the trash bin. Lights atop each of the five pieces of equipment rotated, casting shimmering splashes of eerie light onto the faces of the bystanders who'd pushed themselves as close as they could get to the central attraction. The dead woman quietly surveyed the scene from within her plastic shroud.

"Is that Mazie?" he heard someone ask. "I haven't seen her in weeks. Didn't she pack up and leave the first of May? It can't be her."

"She sure did. Headed back to Bangor like she does every summer. Too hot down here for her. I saw her loading stuff into her car. She looked too scrawny to lift a paper sack, let alone those heavy suitcases." David kept his face stony while he listened and pretended disinterest.

"Her car's gone," someone said. "I'm sure she left."

"Lord Almighty! What's going on here? This is a quiet town. No trouble at all. Even the bars are peaceful hereabouts." That from a tall woman with a man's build.

"You can't say that. Think about the bare-top bikini contests
~~~~~~~~~~~

on Friday nights at Slam Dunk's. I hear the yelling all the way up the beach."

"Yeah, and what about the rowing teams practicing on the river during winter break. They get pretty loud with their megaphones."

"Don't get sarcastic. You know what I mean. No real crime happens here. We're mostly too old and feeble to break any law." Her retort brought a chuckle from the onlookers.

A policeman ran a yellow tape all around the dumpster while his fellow officers took down the names and statements of everyone in the crowd. David assumed it was the medical examiner and two lab techs who busied themselves with the body. Being careful, they wore cloth booties and latex gloves. In this heat their hands must be juicy with sweat. No help for that. David tried to decide who was in charge. A broad-hipped woman with a thick blond plait dangling down her back wore the most gold braid, so he approached her.

"Chief Elston?" he asked. She looked his way, so he added, "I'm David Santorino. I called this in." Her frown deepened.

"I don't like it one bit that you left this woman's body unattended," she said. "You city people may treat human beings like so much carrion. Down here in the Sunshine State we're respectful of our citizens, deceased or not."

"I'm sorry, but my ice cream was melting." What he heard next was a very unladylike snort.

"Ice cream! We have a dead woman and you're only thought was for your groceries? An infant would have more sense. Let's see your ID." She held out her hand, palm up. He felt like a ten-year-old child caught stealing quarters from his mother's purse. She took down every mark on his card then asked, "Why didn't someone else see this woman? She's plainly visible with the lid held up by Saturday's trash from the beach crowd."

"I stopped to watch a raccoon climb into the bin. It tore open the plastic. Before that, you couldn't see her." The chief shook her head and grimaced.

"Those animals get into everything no matter what kind of lid the city constructs. I suppose he was fat."

"The largest raccoon I'd ever seen."

"Get yourself together and give a report. We want anything you saw." He'd seen prickly pears with fewer thorns than this police chief.

"The lot was empty when I drove up. I started toward the unit and saw the raccoon, so I went back to the car for my camera."

"Empty?" She looked around. "I count twenty cars on this side of the building."

"Empty of people. No other persons out here."

"Let's be precise with our language . . . Agent Santorino." She'd glanced down at her clipboard to read her notes before she appended his name to her sentence.

"I sense a truckload of hostility. What's the FBI done for you lately, Chief?"

"I could go on and on, but your damn labs lost me a case this week," Elston said. Her scowl softened into an attractive smile; she reached out to shake David's hand. "Shoot! I shouldn't take it out on you. Linda Elston here." His answering grin froze on his face when she switched moods and added another reprimand. "You probably tromped all over the scene. Better have the techs make a cast of your shoe soles."

"I took off my shoes, felt for a pulse, then backed off a good fifteen feet. She'd slipped past rigor mortis."

"I'd expect more from a champion cop." A sneer replaced her smile. Boy, did she have some chip on her shoulder. He headed for the lab boys and found himself inside the cloud of vile smells emanating from trash and its decomposition. Mazie's body had already attracted a swarm of blue flies. Ashes to ashes and dust to dust, he knew, with hungry maggots in between. He pushed aside thoughts of the flies and their swarming larvae to concentrate on his purpose for being in Sunny Shores.

He'd get reacquainted with his sister, give her a break in the care of his niece and nephew, improve his golf game, and be a vegetable. He'd sit on the balcony and drink beer; mainly he'd lose the strict discipline that edged his life like an electrified strand of barbed wire. He let the tension drop from his shoulders and took a deep breath. This brought a modicum of peace to his spirit even while he stood amidst the frantic activity and high emotions of a pulsing crime scene.

As his mind drifted he saw himself meeting a woman—somebody friendly, uncomplaining, and drop-dead beautiful. She'd smile up at him. Her brown eyes would sparkle. She'd reach out her arms . . . The problem was, she still looked like Mia. It was Mia he held in his arms, Mia he wanted, the Mia who no longer wanted him. He might as well join the body in the trash.

He slammed the door on those thoughts lurking in the forbidden depths of his brain, but he knew the cure for self-pity. He decided to add a daily run to his vacation schedule. When the ME had finished with him, he located his running shoes and jersey shorts. The luminous moon above gave plenty of light for a nighttime run on the blessedly hard, flat beach sand.

Sunday, July 6th

The drive to Orlando on Route 528 was tropical, beautiful, and sinister. The roadside foliage of Florida presents a darker green than the trees and bushes of Kansas or Iowa. He rolled west on a smooth strip of straight concrete with nothing but thick trees and dense underbrush on either side. The contrast between this road and the familiar, crowded freeways streaking into Chicago and Kansas City couldn't have been sharper. Here greenery—there suburban housing, apartment buildings, and old warehouses. Here mostly cars, a few towing boats, a smattering of cement trucks and pickups—there lines of over-size semis with brave sedans wedged in between them. What lurked behind the lush Florida foliage? Probably bobcats and black bears, not to mention alligators. If his car broke down there would be no place to get help, and mosquitoes would be fierce. He promised himself a can of Deep Woods Off to keep in the glove box.

Martha waved as he pulled up outside Southwest's baggage-claim area. God, but it was good to see her familiar smile! A dentists dream! Two rows of white teeth split her face and her blue eyes gleamed with pleasure. Kids and suitcases filled the area around her. As soon as he'd hugged his sister and the children, he loaded their piles of luggage into the trunk of the gray midsized Buick he'd rented.

"Down here you only need a few swim suits and a towel," he said. "It's not the Ritz. Do I count six bags?" He watched her face darken and wondered what he'd said to upset her. Was she getting fragile or something?

"Now don't start off criticizing me," she said. "Most of that is for the kids. You'd be surprised how much stuff they need. When are you going to get some of your own? Kids that is." She had the grace to blush. "David, I'm so sorry. My big mouth; but I never did like Mia, and she certainly didn't take to me."

"It's done, Martha. Over with. Finished." Words he himself could not accept and did not believe. He busied himself helping her secure the children's car seats with safety belts.

"You'll catch yourself a beautiful babe this very week," she said. "I'll see to it. That's what Mom sent me here to do. And me, I do whatever Mama says."

"That'll be the day. You've been screaming insults at her ever since you could stand up in your crib and make it rattle."

"Huh! We get along just fine. What would a man who lives two hundred miles away know about his home-town mom and little sister? And besides, you were always too busy with your weird pals to know what I was up to." By this time they'd left the covered driveway and circled south around the terminal.

Brilliant oleander bushes and lush grass lined either side of the road as David headed for the 528 East exit ramp.

"I rented the condo for us sight unseen. How is it?" she asked.

"Not bad. Perfect view of the ocean, the elevator works, the kitchen is clean, and the TV screen is gigantic." He didn't mention the body in the dumpster.

"Did the management deliver the two cribs I asked for?"

"They put one in each bedroom. Which kid do I sleep with?"

"I'll take the baby—she's still nursing. You get the big shot. Since you two are the oldest in your families, you'll find you have lots in common. He was born bossy. Lucas calls Andrew the general."

"How bout that, general?" He turned his head so his voice would carry to the rear. "Are you and I running the place? We have only two weeks to get these women into line." When he didn't get an answer, Martha turned to look at her offspring.

"I think they fell asleep before we hit the expressway. We had to get up at 4:00 a.m. to reach Des Moines on time for our flight, and they were too excited to sleep on the plane. This will be the most peaceful car ride since I had Andrew." Her words expressed regret, but her face and body language exuded serenity.

"You love it, don't you."

"Mothering kids? I do indeed. They use me up every day. I matter to them. What more could a woman want?"

"How about your career? Don't you miss the excitement of the courthouse?"

"You mean do I miss gut-wrenching failures, last minute no-shows, and daily tangles with judges who only want their calls to be over with?" She paused before she answered her own question. "Actually, some days I do, but I can return when the children are in school. Not many new law-school graduates want public-sector pay. We're lucky to get a third of what the hotshot litigators pull down their first year of practice."

"What made you choose the public defender's office? You ranked right up near the top of your class. You could have gone to work anywhere."

"You crime-fighter guys make mistakes. Lots of them. Somebody needs to give you a hard time, and I'm good at that."

"That you are." They passed through the toll booth, paid their fee, and headed due east toward the Atlantic. "You like to save the little guys," he said, "and I want to take down the big fish. What makes us so antagonistic?"

"Must be all that sweet corn we ate as kids," she said, "or maybe the wide prairies bred some kind of endless tenacity into our souls."

"Do you remember the field corn that grew the other side of our backyard fence? 'Stand up straight,' it always said to me, 'and live tall'."

"I can't believe my big brother listened to the corn rustle and heard entire sentences. No wonder you had weird friends."

"Not weird at all. We were just a very ordinary bunch of guys."

"Yeah? How about the one who played the tuba in the high-school band? He must have had a perennial back ache from lugging that thing around on his belly."

"Jerry Michaels? He's about as ordinary as anyone could get. He teaches band and music in Lost Lake and sends kids to the state contest every year. Now me, I was the weird one. I went out for debate."

"Which surprised no one."

"What did your friends think of your own debating prowess?"

"Easy answer. They all knew I had a mouth." She yawned, and gazed out the window for a few miles. "It's a wonder either one of us has verbal skills, with an accountant for a dad and a math-teacher mom. Is it this desolate all the way to the beach? It could get scary out here if the car broke down."

"Not a good idea, so I'll just keep on rolling. Soon you'll see the bridge that rises over the Indian River. A few miles after that, we cross the Banana River. From then on, it's one hotel after another. Tourist row."

"I'm so excited. Two whole weeks to lie in the sun and play in the ocean. Is there a grill at our condo?"

"That I did get, and I bought the steaks and charcoal to go with it."

"I brought a ton of sun screen."

"So did I. With my skin, I plan to run before sunrise, wear a hat to play golf, and use the afternoon shade on the beach or at the pool to give you a break from your responsibilities."

"That's very generous."

"An uncle should get to know his niece and nephew; but how do I keep the baby from eating sand?" David looked over at Martha when she didn't answer and found she'd followed her children to sleepy land.

Poor kid. I've not heard one word of complaint about being stuck raising the kids by herself, and she must be truly worried with Lucas overseas. Peacekeeping was proving to be pretty hostile. She woke up when he pulled into the lot behind the police station.

"Martha, I have to run in here; it won't take long. I'll leave the AC running." He grabbed the envelope he'd stuck between the front seats and got out.

The chief's offices were upstairs and down a corridor. The decor hailed from the sixties, all gray paint and smoky glass. Her door stood open, so he poked his head in. She had her feet on the desk and was yakking into the phone.

The chief of police in a city of fourteen thousand had plenty of work to do, especially when the population was doubled by winter tourists. She beckoned him in. When he started to put the manila envelope on her desk, she held one hand up, palm forward *alá* traffic cop.

"Got to go," she said into her phone. "Nobody comes in and you don't go out. Got that? And Carlton stays with you every minute." She paused to hear the answer. "I love you too," she said, and hung up.

"My offspring are home from day camp and have to check in with me. One of these days I'll mount surveillance cameras on the perimeter of our property. Every rebellious kid in the neighborhood is dying to get the children of the police chief in trouble. They're good kids but not immune to temptation."

"I'm dropping off the pictures I took. There's a great one of the raccoon, but I don't think it will help. I wrote out a report and had it witnessed by the building manager." He watched a cloud pass briefly across her face and wondered why.

"Thank you," she said. "So how long will you be in our fair city?"

"Two weeks. Call if you need anything more from me."

"You're living with a bunch of old folks. Hope they don't bore you to death. Is this your first time in Sunny Shores?" David nodded.

"It is. We rented sight unseen, and we certainly won't mind some elderly peace and quiet." He was pleased they'd picked a spot with nothing but sand and ocean for miles in either direction. At least Martha wouldn't be hounding him to date the residents. He headed back to his car, relieved to be done with his duty to the local cops.

"What was that all about?" Martha asked. "You've already gotten into trouble with the Sunny Shores police?" She yawned and ran her fingers through her short dark curls.

"I had the misfortune to discover a body in the dumpster last night. The chief would love to pin the crime on me."

"Any stranger would do, right? Keep the locals out of trouble." Martha applied a rosy lipstick, eyeing herself in the mirror on her sun visor.

"That's a problem, since the woman appeared to have died

some time before I arrived. Anyway, I took some pictures and gave her a report. End of the matter. The chief is a real piece of work—looks like Helga the Viking and talks like Attila the Hun."

"Then it shouldn't be hard to stay out of her way."

"Right, and here we are at the Tudor Arms with two weeks of nothing but sun, sand, and time to play with the kids. Fourteen days on the bright side of life."

"See no evil, hear no evil, speak no evil. That's us."

CHAPTER 2

Monday, July 7

David woke at five to the quiet beep of the alarm, drank his coffee, and hit the cool sands of the beach by five-fifteen. He thought he'd try running barefoot so he tied his shoes together and hung them around his neck. In less than a block he discovered broken shells have sharp edges; he stopped to work his sand-encrusted feet back into his socks and shoes.

The eastern sky grew light, exposing a group of dark purple clouds rising like fairy-tale castles on the horizon. A gray mist dimmed the outlines of the buildings to his right. Running across the flat sands of low tide, he noticed someone wrapped in a blanket. Were the homeless a problem in Sunny Shores? Probably. If the time ever came when David couldn't afford the price of shelter, he'd prefer a Florida beach to a cardboard box under Chicago's Randolph Street or a doorway in downtown Kansas City.

He ran south for half an hour and sweated through his shirt and shorts in the rising heat. His arms and legs were slick with his perspiration. It was a bit more pleasant heading north with a light breeze, but he decided to run even earlier the next morning.

The brilliant orange sun hung briefly above the horizon before rising rapidly, all the while aiming a golden arrow across the waters straight at his feet. Looking at the shining path, a person might easily conclude he was the center of the universe.

When he returned, he noticed the outdoor shower and the sign: "Please don't track in sand or tar. Wash your feet or remove your shoes." He did both and sat on the nearby wooden bench to air-dry his feet.

The incoming surf spread serenity into the jagged corners of his mind and the mesmerizing beauty of the ocean absorbed some of his enduring internal ache. Endless rows of white froth and pewter colored water rolled to shore, no two waves ever alike.

The beach began its daily draw of admirers. Old ladies in wide-brimmed hats waded in the surf, stooping now and then to inspect a shell. Two serious runners loped across the damp shoreline.

Half a block away, the rolled up blanket was still there. Wouldn't the guy be sweltering?

~~~~~~~~~~~

Upstairs, Martha had drained the coffee pot, so he made a fresh brew. She already had the kids in their swim suits and was spooning oatmeal into the baby while Andrew ate his Cheerios.

"These two are wired," Martha said, "but it's much too early for their mama."

"I'm going to the beach!" Andrew yelled and waved his spoon toward the seaside glass doors. "I want to make a huge fort." The boy strung out the word "huge" until it became a sentence unto itself.
~~~~~~~~~~~

"Yeah, kid, but be careful with that spoon. We don't want cereal in our eyes. Martha, I don't have a tee time, but I'm sure the starter can find a spot for a single. Will you be okay here without the car? I'll quit after nine holes."

"Play all day if you want to. Life around here is one big sandbox and I'm dying to scoop it up."

"I've got to shower. It's hot already. Do you have water bottles for the kids?"

"David, I'm a pro. The kids look healthy enough, don't they?"

"Yeah, but this is Florida. It's a lot closer to the equator than back home." She shook her head and continued to feed baby Susan.

"It's not any hotter than Iowa. I've been watching the temperatures online. The ocean breeze cools things down in the evening."

"You've got to admit the sun's rays are more direct."

"Your job is to find a woman, not to worry about my kids. Check out the golf course for a likely one who gets long drives, and I'll inspect the beach for prospects. We won't go home empty handed." That stopped him.

"Why long drives?"

"I don't want someone who'll hold us up on the golf course, and she'll need a strong ego to handle herself in our family. That was always Mia's trouble. Too many feelings of inferiority."

Now that gave the federal agent something to think about.

"Do you want me to give Susan a shower? She has more food on the outside than you've managed to shovel in."

"Go on, get out of here. See if you can find a beautiful college professor. We could use a little academic class." She resumed the subject a few minutes later when he'd dressed himself in a polo shirt and shorts.

"And red hair. Just imagine the glow that would add to our family reunion photographs. Yes, she definitely must have red hair." David walked to the windows overlooking the ocean.

"There were fishing boats off-shore when I ran this morning, and a couple of cruise ships waiting to get into port. Now the beach is beginning to acquire families, umbrellas, and surfers."

"I'm sure we won't be alone."

"There's a beach bum still rolled up in a blanket. It's probably some homeless person sleeping off his Chianti."

"I don't like the idea of beach bums or winos around my babies."

"I don't either, so I'll check him out before I leave." He took the back stairs two at a time and plodded across the sand to crouch beside the sleeper.

"Excuse me, sir. Are you all right? You've been out here a long time. Maybe you should find a place in the shade." At first David spoke softly to the covered form. He felt like a museum visitor talking to a mummy and looked around with embarrassment to see if anyone heard him. No part of the person showed. Maybe a joke. Somebody wrapped up pillows to make it look like a body. He felt foolish, but hell, he couldn't leave for the golf course with potential harm to his niece and nephew lurking on the beach.

Feeling uneasy, he lifted a corner of the blanket. Not another black plastic bag! It did look like a body. No rise and fall to the chest region. Mustn't touch. That would leave fingerprints. He pulled a cell phone from his pocket and dialed 911, grateful he'd been able to spare Martha and the children from stumbling upon this grim scene.

A small crowd had gathered by the time the beach patrol and police emergency truck arrived. Chief Elston came toward him, looking hot and uncomfortable in her twill shirt.

"What the hell is it with you? You come down here to plague me?" David stood to meet her.

"I don't know what we have here, Chief. Could be a joke. I didn't want to touch anything and have tried to keep bystanders back. This bundle was here when I ran at five-thirty. I just came down to look because he didn't move when the sun climbed and the temperature rose." What was it about this woman that made him so defensive? He babbled like a school kid caught lighting fires in the john.

"I brought an evidence tech, and he's complaining like hell. You kept him up most of Saturday night with that body in the dumpster."

~~~~~~~~~~~

The white-coated tech pulled on gloves and knelt to slit the bag open as an assistant made notes. Those standing nearby gasped. Thin gray hair covered a woman's skull. Her eyes were slightly open. As the scissors moved farther down the plastic bag, David noticed the painful thinness of her arms. Someone behind him spoke.

"That's Miriam. She lives in the condo. My God! She looks like she just staggered out of Dachau."

~~~~~~~~~~~

"Do you think we should find another place to stay?" David asked Martha later. "Maybe in another town?"

The police had questioned everybody and had gone off with the body. His sister sat on the beach beside the baby's portable playpen, while David helped Andrew build a castle with a moat. They'd already constructed a three-story structure with corner turrets. Now Andrew ran back and forth carrying dripping pails of water to fill the moat.

"I do not." Martha adjusted the beach umbrella shade Susan. "The dead women have nothing to do with us. Besides, I signed a contract for two weeks and paid in advance. I'm not giving money away even if it is yours. You should go on and play golf. We'll be fine here."

"Yeah, sure."

"What's with that Chief Elston? She seems to have it in for you."

"She hates the FBI and detests me for finding the one in the dumpster. Now she has another reason to."

"She'll get over it." Martha scanned a local paper she'd picked up in the hall. "Now here's a good idea. There's a fishing pier nearby that extends over the ocean. It has shops and restaurants. We ate the steaks, and I didn't see any other meat in the refrigerator. Let's try dinner on the pier."

"Fine."

"Would you believe the prices are cheaper if you arrive before six o'clock? They call it the Early-bird Special. My kids eat early anyway."

"That we can do." Andrew returned with another bucketful and poured it into their trench. As the water disappeared into the sand, the boy's shoulders sagged and his lower lip protruded.

"I want him to float." Andrew said. He gripped a plastic alligator.

"Tomorrow we'll build our castle closer to the water's edge. It's too dry this far up the beach."

"He needs water," the boy insisted.

"What about digging deeper?" Martha asked. "Would you strike water? We can't be much above the water table."

"Maybe, but here's what we will do. I'll find some plastic to line our moat so the water won't sink in. Hold off a bit with the bucket brigade, okay, Sport?" Andrew grinned and tried to bite a hole in his uncle's leg with the toy reptile.

~~~~~~~~~~~

Inside the dimly lit first-floor hallway where David went to look for a plastic bag, he overheard a voice.

"This has got to stop!" Was that Chief Elston? He saw her broad back and the blond braid in the doorway of the
~~~~~~~~~~~

manager's unit. She yelled at whoever was inside. "You know Mother won't stand for it." She looked down the hall, spotted David, and yanked the door shut behind her. He wasn't breaking any law he knew of by loitering outside to listen.

"Just what we need," he heard. "A fucking FBI agent. Whatever possessed you to rent a unit to that nosey supercop?" The chief's harangue could pass through solid wood planking, but with the glass sidelight and hollow doors, she might as well have been equipped with a megaphone.

"You want the unit to sit empty?" The manager's words were harder to understand. David pressed his ear to the door, swiveling his eyes from the elevator doors to the two ground-level entries. "Using electricity? Soaking up the tax reserves? I do the best I can. Besides, I rented to a Mrs. Martha Homemaker with two kids. Didn't know shit about her brother. It's mine now, and I can't afford dead weight."

"What do you mean, 'mine'. You've got about as much claim as I have, maybe less," the chief said.

"Quick and Easy Cash is my baby. I thought it up. I loaned the money."

"Money you didn't have. Money I gave you."

"Miriam had good jewelry and a huge TV, not to mention my security interest in her condo."

"That didn't offset her medical bills. You've got to keep the others alive, or at least sell them burial insurance."

"Hell, I wish the tide had swept her out to sea."

"Hell yourself. You're a surfer. You know everything comes to shore sooner or later. Even you drifted back in that time the shark took a bite and left in disgust. Where *were* you when God passed out brains?"

"I didn't . . . " The door knob turned and David fled.

~~~~~~~~~~~
~~~~~~~~~~~

He returned to his family carrying wide strips of plastic he'd cut from a dry-cleaning bag. He'd brought his navy summer jacket, which still smelled of harsh solvents. Did people wear jackets down here? Martha deserved at least one expensive dinner at a white-tablecloth restaurant.

It took awhile for David and Andrew to construct a waterproof liner for the moat, time he spent imagining possible conclusions to the conversation he'd overheard between Chief Elston and the building manager.

~~~~~~~~~~~

"It's not every day an Iowa girl gets to view the Atlantic Ocean while she eats her way through a mound of boiled shrimp," Martha said. She dipped the lovely pink-and-white meat into red sauce and popped it into her mouth. "And I can't believe this wonderful ocean breeze."

"It's a gale," David said, "fighting to turn our paper napkins into beach litter." He'd just finished spooning applesauce into Susan's mouth, a moving target. Andrew was doing pretty well with the hot dog Martha had cut into small pieces. "I don't know which to watch: the babes and muscle men playing volleyball or the elegant surfers." Susan banged her heels against the footrest of her high chair. "Look at the little kids sliding on boogie boards. We should get Andrew one."

"He's too young, but since you're interested, you could take surfing lessons. We drove past a school on the way here."

"We could both do it."

"That we could, but don't look now," Martha said. "There's a gorgeous woman watching you."

"Come off it, Martha."

"I'm not kidding, and I think I've seen her before."

"You've been in Sunny Shores barely twenty-four hours. There's no way you could recognize anybody. This isn't Podunk, Iowa."
~~~~~~~~~~~

"Don't be such a snob about your home town. It was good to you. Even if I haven't seen her around our condo, she has to be the college professor we're looking for."

"College professors don't go for FBI types. They're too liberal to believe in law and order. And she's beyond pretty; she wouldn't be allowed to attend faculty meetings with all the stringy vegetarians and pudgy frumps."

"At least you're looking at a woman. That's a good start. Did you notice how expensive her clothes look? And she must have three thousand dollars wrapped around her neck. I've never seen so much gold."

"What I see is the sketch pad she just pulled from her tote bag." Her pencil whipped across the paper, but he wasn't near enough to see what shape the lines took. "She looks great in that blue linen suit but overdressed for an outdoor bar."

"Should we have dessert?"

"Sure. Some ice cream? I'm planning to put on a few pounds."

"I'm not." Martha said. "I bought a swim suit one size too small, and I'm getting into it come hell or high water. But if you beg, I'll split a chocolate sundae."

"There's a DQ on the way back to our condo. How about a Peanut Buster?"

"Oh, boy! You really pushed the right button there. The DQ was our favorite high-school hangout. That's where I met Lucas. He always gave me extra chocolate fudge topping and double whipped cream to prove his devotion. That's what made my arms so plump."

"Your arms bear witness to Mom's meatloaf and Dad's scalloped potatoes. The DQ and Lucas must account for your forty-pound earlobes."

Her glare should have sent him away whimpering.

Tuesday, July 8th

The next morning David ran early. By sunrise he was taking

his second cup of coffee and his bowl of sugar-free cereal to the balcony, where Martha joined him.

"The kids are both asleep. I don't know what I'm doing awake at six," she said.

"The ocean's beautiful. It's well worth getting out of bed to soak up the poetry."

"You're right. Every little cloud is painted a brilliant shade of pink; they look incredibly soft." Martha examined the beach. "David, take your eyes off of the horizon and look down. She's there, the woman from the pier restaurant."

A blonde and a small boy shoveled sand into a heap right in front of their building. She worked with vigor, looked strong, and did a nice job of filling out her bikini. "What do you think they're doing?"

"Digging for treasure." He picked up the binoculars.

"Or maybe starting a sand sculpture. I saw that done on Waikiki on our honeymoon. Lucas took pictures of a perfect sand mermaid before the ocean reclaimed its own."

"This one could be a mermaid, too. The sand pile is shaped like a question mark."

"It looks like they're pretty near the high-tide line. Look, she's backing off. You'd think she'd seen a ghost."

"She did." David shoved the glasses toward Martha and ran from the balcony. When she had them focused properly she saw what he'd seen. A stiff hand protruding from the trench the woman and boy had dug. Just then David reopened the glass doors. "Call 911. Chief Elston doesn't want to hear from me again." Then he was gone; Martha appreciated his remembering not to shout.

He raced across the sand to the incipient sculpture, gave the woman a curt nod, and knelt to inspect the body.

Carolyn Brockton reached for her son, more to reassure herself than to comfort him. This had to be the man she'd seen at the restaurant, the one so inept at feeding his own baby daughter. She felt sorry for the child's mother. He acted like he'd never met the kids, but she couldn't miss the boy's resemblance to him. Same fair coloring, same long eyelashes. How heartless could a father be? And she'd overheard the couple argue about who should pay the bill as they walked past her table. If that wasn't a strange relationship! Even so, he'd carried the boy on his shoulders and bought each child a huge dolphin-shaped balloon. Now here he was, shoving her aside and taking charge. That she particularly hated.

He took her shovel and began to probe the sand, no doubt seeking the outline of the body. She felt like yelling at him, but she shrank from dealing with whatever might lie beneath the surface. She moved back and pulled her son away from the spot that had so recently seemed benign and familiar.

A few other early risers stopped to watch, and now part of the arm was exposed, the rest of the body covered by a black plastic bag. God! Why did she pick this particular spot to dig in? She remembered; it had been slightly raised and she decided it would cut the amount of time and effort needed to build the dragon she'd promised Timmy.

Carolyn Brockton had been creating sand sculpture since a high-school teacher had introduced her to the art form. It always drew a crowd. It was even a sad kind of pleasure to watch the ocean eat away her work, although today's product might have lasted longer. The spot she'd chosen was pretty close to the thin row of rust-colored sea grass that marked the high tide line. She often earned money for her efforts. Some hotels liked to entertain their guests with sand sculptures—but not today and not in front of her dad's building. She grabbed her camera from its case and began to take pictures.

"Good idea," David said. "The police should be here shortly. Can you keep on taking shots? I left my camera upstairs." Her look was cool; David felt stung by her silent criticism. "You don't talk much, do you?" he asked.

"You don't give a person much of a chance." Her voice had softer tones than the flat speech of his own Midwest upbringing. Tennessee? The Carolinas?

"Sorry." He stood and extended his hand. "I'm David Santorino, FBI." One of the high and mighty, she thought. No wonder he exuded as much arrogance as a British peer.

"Struggling artist and full-time hippie, here." She said it to tease him, to put them on opposite sides of the social spectrum. It served him right for being so bossy. She allowed him to look directly into her eyes and flushed slightly at his very masculine approval. His eyes dropped to focus on her gold chains. Damn! They were expensive. Of its own volition, one hand rose to cover them.

"You don't shovel sand like a hippie," he said. "What I saw was energy and purpose." He resumed probing and scraped a line that had begun to take the shape of a human form. They were silent, listening to the whispers and gasps from the people behind them. He hoped the police would arrive soon and without their chief—wishes soon to be denied.

When the ME had slit the plastic to expose the face, Carolyn moaned. She dropped to her knees in the sand; her fingers digging white dents in the skin of her thighs.

"No! Not our Agnes. It can't be Agnes!"

Chief Linda knelt beside her. "You could be right, she said. "I haven't seen her in ages."

"She's so thin." Carolyn sat back on her heels and studied the body. "Remember how soft and loving she was? A warm hug and cookies every day after school, and angel food cakes for our birthdays."

"She's not eaten any cookies or cakes for months," Linda said, "judging by the lack of body fat."

"Don't you go technical on me. What happened? I've been too damn busy with my damn career. How could we let this happen to Agnes?"

"She's not our responsibility."

"Like hell she's not! You don't take all that love and not give it back. She's the one who got us through Mom's first divorce."

The ME had stopped working. He sat back on his haunches and watched Carolyn and Linda. David, too, focused on the dramatic interplay. Attila the Hun and Carolyn had had the same babysitter? The same mother? He noted the blond hair, the blue eyes—both pairs now fierce and defiant—the wide mouths and tan skin. Could be, though Linda outweighed Carolyn by fifty pounds and had the balls of a bull.

The body was forgotten by all who watched save the ME, who resumed his careful inspection. Linda sighed and drew her sister into her capable arms.

"You're right honey, but I still wish she'd chosen to die on someone else's beach." Linda stood and brushed the sand from her knees. "And as for you, Mr. FBI, did you haul bodies down in a pickup truck to dump your case load into my peaceful little cotton patch?"

~~~~~~~~~~~

By the time Linda's scorching lecture ended and the ME left, David was sore enough to toss his golf clubs into the ocean. He headed for his car, trying futilely to recall a mantra for peace he'd learned during the years of his youth when he'd explored various eastern religions. "Forgive us our sins," he managed to mutter, "as we forgive . . . "

~~~~~~~~~~~

The sight in the parking lot brought him up short. A colorful old Volkswagen bus squatted on the pavement. My God, the lady is a hippie! Not an inch could be seen of the original paint. He walked around to inspect all four sides. Palm trees, pelicans, a lemon tree, and two soaring dolphins adorned the rounded surfaces; a red sunset splashed across the rear doors. Even the bumpers boasted a tropical scene.

"It's a beauty, isn't it." He turned toward Carolyn's voice. The small boy fidgeted beside his mother, hopping from one foot to the other.

"Did you paint this?" David asked.

"I wish I had. I'm trying to get my department to buy it for the lobby of our new building—it's a terrific example of original Florida art. I'll sculpt a sand alligator in front of it and put up a sign that says, 'Southernmost spot in the U.S.'" She laughed, which only added to his puzzlement.

"I don't get it."

"You Yankees! Haven't you ever seen a conch car?" He shook his head and continued to stare. "They're a product of Key West, and I'm convinced of their historic value. In these prosperous times the art is dying out. People are too busy making money to be creative."

"That body you discovered didn't look prosperous. Did you know your Agnes is the third emaciated dead woman found here? The police hate me."

"With good reason. Murder headlines are bad for tourism."

"I disagree. Crime news will bring as many crowds to the beach as free beer. What were you drawing last night?" She blushed. Intent on her sketch, she'd not been aware of his attention.

"Surfers. Their sleek bodies make beautiful contrasting lines against the froth of the sea. I thought you were too busy playing at being a daddy to notice anything else."

"You'd be hard for any red-blooded male to miss." That sent ice through her veins. Did he flirt with every woman he met? She felt hot pity for his wife and turned to the wagon.

"It's time for Timmy's swim class. I hope you enjoy your visit to Florida." Damn! Such a polite Southern woman. She wished she'd not encouraged his interest.

"Martha would love to meet you. She's a home-bound mom and you know that gets lonesome." She slammed her door and drove off. What was he? One of those guys who liked three in a bed?

David wondered what her name was and what he'd done to rouse her anger. He'd have to check the police reports. They'd interviewed her, but he hadn't been near enough to catch the details. He made a mental note of her license plate, not that anybody could miss the rolling gallery of Caribbean art.

She was obviously related to the police chief. Did that make her a local? But no matter what Martha wanted, he wasn't about to get interested in a woman who lived twelve hundred miles from his present assignment.

He headed for the golf course.

There he learned it would be twenty minutes before the starter could work him in with another single and a twosome. He plunked his quarters into the proper slot and hit a bucket of balls at the driving range while waiting for his name to be called. The heat was fierce, and it wasn't even ten yet. How long had it been since he'd played golf? A year? Two? His boss had been nagging him about getting out on Sunday mornings as a sub in a regular foursome. He needed to sharpen his game. This looked like a simple course. He could relax.

The snippy hippie sand sculptor turned out to be the other single.

"I suppose we could split the cost and share a cart," she said. "Are you a safe driver?"

"You'll find out." He gestured to the padded bench beside him and zoomed toward what he thought was the first tee.

"Wrong," she said. "We're starting on the river course."

"You drive." He wanted to add something nasty, like, "You think you're so smart," but of course he was too mature for such petulance. When she out-drove and under-putted him on the first two holes, he lost all grip on maturity.

"A bit rusty, aren't you," she said. "Where did you learn to play golf?"

"In Iowa. Elmwood Country Club."

"I know. You're rich and your daddy is a doctor."

"An accountant, and I worked as a caddy. Good tips, and it got me a golf scholarship at the university."

"Don't be so touchy. We Southerners have learned to be cool."

"The weather's so blasted hot you have to carry ice around on your shoulder." Stinging sweat ran into his eyes and dripped off the tip of his nose.

"No, that's where we carry the bitterness left over from the Civil War, and we magnolias have sense enough to keep the sweat out of our eyes with a bandana." He glanced at her. She did indeed have a kerchief tied across her forehead under the wide brim of her hat. "You need to stop in at the clubhouse to buy a sweat band. Why did you leave your wife at the condo with the kids? Are you some kind of cave man throwback?" Now that was interesting; she assumed Martha was his wife.

"She ordered me off to the golf course. Says that's the only way she's getting any peace on this vacation." It was definitely fun to live a lie. "Martha is the breeding-kids kind. Me, I like a woman of the world." He ogled her with his eyebrows wiggling up and down.

She didn't speak for the next four holes.

"We're tied," he said. "Want to put five bucks on the next hole?"

"You're on." It worked out his way by one stroke. She dug around in her golf bag and him handed the money when they reached their cart.

"Want to try to win it back?" he said.

"You think you've been sandbagged?"

"I'm sure of it."

"Then let's play for ten."

"Let's play for steaks. I'll grill, you buy."

Carolyn waited for him to tee up on the men's tee, then shot a perfect drive down the middle of the fairway with a good chance to chip onto the green and par the hole with two putts.

"I think you'll buy and you'll grill," she said.

~~~~~~~~~~~

"We'll see you at seven?" he said later in the parking lot. "That way we'll have time to visit while the steaks cook."

"Won't Martha mind you bringing a guest?"

"She'll love your company. She's a very social person."

"But you're not?" He lifted his clubs into the trunk before answering.

"I've been called a loner, among other things."

"So have I."

"Two of a kind. Do you vote independent?"

"That question is much too personal."

"I'll return the cart." He changed shoes and drove off a little too fast, hoping she watched, recognizing a fool when he was one.
~~~~~~~~~~~

CHAPTER 3

When Carolyn came to the door that evening, she wore a pale blue sleeveless dress and carried a bottle of red wine.

"Made right here in Florida," she said. "Over near Gainesville. It's a fairly good dessert wine."

"Carolyn's Vineyard," he read. "Is that your other business?"

"The vintner named it after his beloved wife, my grandmother."

"I had no idea Florida produced wine." Martha inspected the label. "I think of oranges and grapefruit."

"Don't forget tomatoes, cattle, racehorses, and strawberries, though now most of the tomatoes come from points farther south. There are growers in our state who desperately hate both Clinton and Bush for NAFTA."

"Are you one of them?" David asked.

"I told you. Politics are too personal. Where are you two from?"

"Iowa," Martha said.

"Kansas City," David said, then he grinned. An apologetic smile had served him well in the past, usually sufficient to disarm the stoniest heart.

"Can't you two even get your address straight? I happen to know for certain that Kansas City is not in Iowa. You're a very weird couple."

"David asked me to lie, but I'm truly not good at deception. We grew up in Iowa and David ran off after college." Carolyn flushed at that damning revelation and glared at David.

"You left her with two kids? How awful!" David walked toward Martha and put his arm around her shoulder.

"Meet my kid sister, and the best brains in the family." Carolyn's eyes narrowed.

"I thought it would be safe to come here for dinner, you two married and all."

"What kind of safety are you in need of?" Martha asked.

"Man safety. It's hard to relax. Your husband—I mean your brother—was so obvious I figured him for harmless."

"Have you tried wearing mumu's and a head scarf?"

"I certainly have, but that's not easy in this heat."

"Speaking of heat," Martha said, "could we take our drinks outside? I think the evenings here are wonderful. We don't get cooling evening breezes in Iowa, and we certainly don't have an ocean view." Their guest followed Martha to the balcony where the table was set for three.

"I notice you have binoculars on the ready. Is that how you saw the hand I uncovered this morning?" Carolyn shivered at the gruesome memory.

"It is," David said. "I like to inspect the cruise ships."

"Now why did I assume you watched the pelicans, terns, and skimmers?"

"Skimmers? You mean people here wear those old-time straw hats?"

"No. I mean the black-and-white birds that fly just above the water with their beaks open to scoop their food from the sea. They have red spots on rather large beaks."

"I've not seen anything like that," David said.

"They're very fast and look a bit like gulls or terns in the early morning light. Watch for small flocks of low-flying birds. Actually they might have moved north by now."

"Do you live here full time?" Martha asked.

"No. I came over to check on my dad's condo. He's in Maine for the summer, enjoying the mosquitoes."

"David said you knew the lady you found under the sand."

"Knew her and loved her dearly." Carolyn stared down into the glass in her hand. "I can't get the image of her desiccated body out of my mind."

"What do you think is going on?" Martha asked. "Three dead women in as many days."

"I sat in on a condominium association meeting with Dad a year ago the past spring. Everybody was upset about the new balconies, protesting that they couldn't afford them, screaming about usurious interest rates. That's the only problem I know of."

"This building doesn't look old enough to need a new anything," David said.

"It was built more than twenty-five years ago. Salt air eats into the rebar, and they're what keep the balconies from crumbling."

"I remember the house my folks built," Martha said. "I watched the workmen place rows of metal bars into a wooden form before they poured cement for the front porch. Is that what you mean by rebar?"

"It is. The rebar may last forever in Iowa, but here the concrete gets minute cracks and brine works its way in to create havoc."

"Salt is part of the wonderful smell of the ocean," David said.

"Wonderful, yes, unless your balcony assessment amounts to more than a year's pension."

"I don't see how that could relate to murder," Martha said.

"I can't either," Carolyn said. "There must be another factor." David stood.

"Could I fix you two another drink before I put the steaks on?" he asked. He lifted the lid to inspect the fire. "The coals are ready."

"I'll pass, thank you," Carolyn said.

"None for me," Martha said.

"Steaks, then." David went inside.

"What did you do with the kids?" Carolyn asked. "They're pretty quiet."

"I fed them an early supper and found a grandma type to baby sit. She'd posted a card in the lobby. She looked capable and said she'd keep them until nine. Where's your Timmy?"

"With my sister's kids. They treat him like a teddy bear, and he's young enough not to care." David returned and slid the meat onto the rack.

"Is everybody related down here?" he asked. "Your chief of police told me the mayor is her mother."

"Mine, too."

"So Linda Elston is your sister." David paused to look at Carolyn. "You're nothing alike."

"True. She got all the grit and determination."

"And you got the looks." Carolyn examined her hands and flushed slightly.

"Mother has both. At fifty, she could still be a magazine cover girl. Linda and I are more jealous of her than of each other."

"So, your dad is married to the mayor?" Martha said.

"Was. Past tense. They split years ago."

"Isn't he uncomfortable living in her town?"

"It's his town. His father was an early developer who owned most of the beach-front property and acres of orange groves on the mainland."

"That's impressive," Martha said.

"Big time locally, but that's it. Let's talk about Martha and David for a change. I'm uncomfortable talking about my family."

"Our history won't take long," Martha said. "I'm an army wife—married my high school sweetheart right out of college. He had an ROTC scholarship to get his degree in accounting and went to work in my dad's office. This year he was called up for active duty."

"Oh, my. Not what I thought at all."

"What was that?"

"First off, I thought you and David were married. I was a little afraid you wanted a *ménage à trois* when he asked me to dinner. I also decided David was a terrible husband and father. He paid too much attention to other women and didn't seem to know his own kids."

"That's what Lucas will be like when he returns. Susan won't know him at all."

"I guess one shouldn't be so quick to jump to conclusions."

"Speaking of conclusions, I should serve the steaks. How about the potatoes and salad, Marty?"

"Coming up, Buddy."

"Are those your needle names?"

"The very ones. Do you have brothers, Carolyn?" The change in her face was remarkable. Her lips flattened and her eyebrows dipped downward.

"One. He lives right here in the building. As a matter of fact, he's the manager." David remembered Linda's yelling at him.

"What did he get?" Carolyn looked puzzled. "I mean, you got the looks and Linda got the grit," Martha said. "What did that leave for your brother?"

"Not much, I'm afraid. He certainly lacks determination. Dad put him in charge here, but that's not working out. He's mainly good at surfing."

"Would he help newbies? We both took lessons this afternoon but could use more help."

"He'd do anything for a buck." She stabbed her fork into the steak and sliced vigorously. Her knife shrieked as it scraped against the plate. "Oops! I guess I shouldn't cut meat and talk about my brother at the same time." She chewed. "Terrific! What's in the marinade?"

"Soy sauce, red wine, and garlic salt."

"Where did you learn to cook?"

"Our mother taught each of us to fix our favorite meals. That way she could grade papers until dinner was ready."

"Your family sounds so normal. Is it possible you really like each other?" This time she was careful not think about her brother as she sliced her meat.

Wednesday, July 9th

Byron Brockton looked from the printout to the first rays of light in the east. God, what was his mother thinking when she made Linda chief of police? He brushed damp hair off of his forehead. His straw-colored pony tail was too sun dried and stiff to stay within the constraints of the shoelace he'd tied around it a day or so earlier.

Since Chief Linda had stormed in and issued her latest threat, he'd alternated squinting at his computer screen with a dozen trips to the refrigerator. The nearby wastebasket reeked from the rising pile of empty Coors cans. He'd crushed the last few in his fist so they wouldn't roll out onto the carpet. Sometime during the night he'd taken a short snooze in front of the TV.

His computer work had gone nowhere. The business paid out more than it took in. The bottom line was a net loss getting close to ninety thou. He had to sell the three condos he now more-or-less owned, but then everything would go public and neither Linda nor the mayor would like that. Not to mention the other tenants. He could see the headlines: ***MAYOR'S SON INDICTED FOR PREDATORY LENDING AND MURDER; POLICE CHIEF ELSTON CLAIMS IGNORANCE***. He wrapped his hands around imaginary bars and rattled them, getting the feel of prison. He could hear the clang of metal gates closing behind him.

But he hadn't been predatory at all. Just trying to help out those widows who couldn't pay their balcony assessments. They'd been happy to quit claim their condos to him in exchange for cash and the right to live in their units until they died. Problem was, they didn't die soon enough, and he had to pay their condo bills in the meantime.

He raised his eyes again and looked out the window. Surfing might be good. A few early dudes tested the curl. He was out of here. No need to change clothes; he wore swim trunks day and night and had since he'd quit high school. His stomach pushed up a mighty and satisfying belch. Never mind about the beer. He could out-surf the best, drunk or sober. Holding on to money might not be his thing, but catching waves most certainly was.

It was midsummer and ninety degrees, yet off shore winds had churned up the cool bottom layer of the ocean and tossed it to the beach. His beach. His now-chilly beach. The incessant sough of the waves wove peace into his spirit as he knelt to wax his board. Soon he'd be balancing and gliding, toes hanging, joyously and free of all problems. Man was meant to live by and in the sea. Anybody who could did.

"Hello Byron. What's on your mind? You seem serious this morning." Byron looked up into the face of the FBI agent who'd rented unit 507. The nosey son of a bitch. He should go back to catching the real crooks in Kansas City and leave Sunny Shores alone. "I hear you're top dog on this beach," the agent added. Bryon softened, happy to enjoy the nice respect he heard in the tenant's voice.

"Maybe, but the young ones are closing in."

"That's the way it is everywhere."

"You coming in? I guess you've rented that board with plans to use it." Was that a challenge, the glove thrown down?

"It's mine for a week. Martha and I took lessons yesterday.

So far I've learned this sport is vastly more difficult than it appears."

"Come on in. The water's free." Maybe he could find a nice strong riptide for this snoop to drown in. Get some peace back into his life.

"Thanks. I'm not too crazy about being out here alone. You see any sharks lately?"

"Aw, they don't like the taste of human flesh. There's not much danger if you don't dangle your legs and toes so the big fish think they're silvery little edibles. I don't see any shiny metal wrapped around your ankles or wrists. That's good. I don't know why some idiots get into the ocean with lures tied to their limbs." Byron waded into the sea, then stooped to fasten his ankle strap. The cold water collided with the Coors and overcame it. "It's shallow for quite a ways, so paddle on out if you're strong enough."

David fastened his own strap and awkwardly picked up his board and began to slosh against the incoming waves. His right foot caught on the strap and he nearly fell.

"That tether takes a bit of getting used to," Byron said. Shit, was he stuck with a stupid beginner? He hoped the guy wouldn't get in his way. "I'll try not to ram into you, but you need to look out for other surfers."

"That's what my coach said yesterday. Don't get hit in the head, especially not by a sharp acrylic board."

A whack on the head might be just what you need, Mr. G-man. Byron caught the first good wave and rode a curving path back and forth across it nearly to shore, did a one-eighty and stepped off gracefully. Nothing felt better than a good ride.

David tried a half-second later. He gripped the sides of the undulating platform with both hands, placed his toes at the end of the board, and attempted the leap into the proper mid-board stance, body facing three-quarters to the side. The idea inside his head was perfect, his execution a bit less so.

His board flipped, tumbling him head-first into the sandy bottom; he came up spitting brine. The incredible force of the retreating wave sucked him backwards. Gasping, he grabbed for the board and slid his torso onto its slippery surface. He'd rented a foam board, which was safer for beginners, but the damn thing bounced on the water like an empty Styrofoam cup.

"Keep at it," Byron yelled. "You'll get it next time." Boy was it nice to see the FBI take a fall. He wished for Hawaii and the fifty-footers. Now that would knock the guy over. Maybe he'd stick around and watch. The responsible surfer in him warred with his mean streak. What if he helped? Would the fed cut him some slack?

Naaah. The agent was just down here on vacation like all the rest of the sunburned summer crowd. He'd not been assigned to Byron's case. Or had he? He'd heard the boys up in Tallahassee were working on legislation to stop predatory lending. Stirring up more trouble for honest folk trying to make a living was what they do best. Hell, who was he to know if he'd broken any laws? The old man said to take care of things, and he had.

Linda had no cause to yell at him.

Byron glanced toward the blur on one side. No shit! The dude was up and got a little ride. But he forgot to keep his knees bent and soon slid off. Not bad. Not bad at all. Byron felt the next big one coming, climbed aboard, and tipped into the curve. He doubted there'd be much chance to surf in prison.

For the next hour neither man gave business a thought. At last they flopped onto the warm sand beside their boards, two men at peace with the universe.

"They should make the marines do this in basic," David said. "It's more grueling than the rope climb. Every inch of muscle burns."

"It's better than Zen for relaxation and beats Mary Jane all to hell." Byron coughed. "Sorry. Didn't mean that. Don't know a girl by that name. Never met her and don't want to."

"I'm on vacation. See no evil, hear no evil, speak no evil."

Byron pictured the three bronze monkeys his late Uncle Clyde had kept on his desk. "Silence!" they advised, and he couldn't agree more; his mouth, however, babbled on about his favorite subject.

"Best damn beach anywhere. Hard sand, good bars, gorgeous babes. We've got everything right here on a perfect seventy-two- mile strand. You ever been to Slam Dunks?"

"No."

"Best hamburgers, best women; and best of all, you can work on your tan while you're having lunch."

"We'll have to try it."

"Little kids love the stage. They climb on it and do their jerky little dances. Some of them sing. It keeps them entertained while adults savor their suds."

"You're full of information. Did you ever think about running a travel agency?"

"I spend my entire life on the beach, the part of life that matters. Everybody thinks I should get a real job. Shit, no."

"That's right. Don't work. Just surf."

Byron watched David slide into sleep and picked up his board. Let the guy burn. He deserves it. Teach him to fuck with Florida.

~~~~~~~~~~~

Martha looked down from the balcony five stories above the beach. At least her brother hadn't drowned. It was her turn now. He'd have to wake up and watch the kids as soon as they'd eaten breakfast. She had spent the previous hour on the internet, chatting with friends back home, with her mother, but mainly with Lucas. He lived! Each e-mail she received announced his safety in the subject line.

Lucas, ever the accountant, had an idea about the bodies on the beach. Senior scams, he called it. Countless fly-by-night
~~~~~~~~~~~

entities prey on the elderly. The women had probably lost their savings to some fraudulent investment scheme and had no money left for food. He told her about a pastor on the gulf coast of Florida who had worked through the members of his large Evangelical Church and managed to scour up several million dollars before getting caught.

She should chat with her neighbors, find out if someone in the building had sold them bad insurance or bad investments. But no, she was on vacation. Neither she nor David should get involved with anything even remotely close to crime. Her mind was clear, but her lawyerly blood sizzled with excitement at the prospect of sleuthing.

She heard a determined squeal from the bedroom. Time to feed Susan. She took one last look at the waves curling ashore and imagined the pull of the surf against her legs, the sand gently slipping from beneath her feet as the wave retreated. Yesterday's lesson had been great fun. She looked forward to being on her own in the surf even as she hurried toward her bedroom.

"Mama's coming, sweetie." she crooned. "It's chow time for the best baby girl ever."

~~~~~~~~~~~

Later David worked with Andrew building a new sand castle while Susan played with her toes. He watched his sister stride in from the surf with the world's widest grin plastered across her happy face.

"Martha, you're getting up nearly every time. What are you doing right that I'm not?" She flopped onto her beach towel and waited for sufficient breath to answer.

"Did you ever consider the laws of physics? I'm lighter, not to mention better coordinated. You used to laugh at my ballet classes and cheerleading stunts. Laugh no more!"
~~~~~~~~~~~

"I hope you're about ready to call it quits. Susie has a poopy diaper."

"And here I thought FBI agents could handle any emergency."

Martha stood and returned to the ocean feeling madly in love with the surf board she carried. As she rode in the next time, she watched David plod across the sand toward the building with Suzie gripped under one arm in a football carry and her playpen clutched under the other. Andrew trailed behind him, dragging a beach towel and his shovel. With them gone, she had time for beach sitting. She spotted the woman who'd baby-sat for her and recognized an opportunity for serious gossip.

"Hello, Wanda. How are you?" The woman lowered a paperback book to her chest and peered over the top of her dark glasses.

"You should certainly ask about my health, what with all the dying going on around here. Thank God I didn't borrow money from Byron Brockton." The lady had more bulges than a pregnant sow, and very little of them were concealed beneath the orange-flowered, two-piece swim suit. She could be a line backer, judging from the torso that extended upward from the low-slung canvas beach chair and the thick legs that stuck out in front of her. She must be six feet tall. One very big mama!

"Byron lends out money?" Martha pulled her chair closer to the babysitter and wondered if Wanda was as strong as she looked.

"Quick and Easy Credit. He has a big banner outside his office on A1A. He passed out flyers to everybody in the building right after we got our balcony assessment. There's something fishy around here, and he's the one who smells the rankest. Not that our honorable mayor doesn't have a suspicious odor of her own."

"Are you sure I'm not crashing a soap opera?"

"Lovely beach, ugly corpses?"

"Something like that."

"Frankly," Wanda said, "I'd rather read about murder than have it erupt like adolescent acne in my own building." She tapped the back of her novel. "See this? The killer has offed four prepubescent blonde girls in the first twenty pages, leaving them with roses in their hands. It's quite scary." Martha scanned the lurid cover: *Sunflower*, by Martha Powers. The petals wept blood. With that first name, she must be a good writer. "I'll let you read it next," Wanda added.

"Great. I'll be waiting."

"I read about a book a day," Wanda said. "What else is there to do? Wait to die?"

"In this paradise? I think not."

"I belong to a mystery club and get four new ones a month. Then there's the library with an entire wall of mysteries. At this rate, I could become an expert on solving crimes."

"When did the mystery here begin?" Martha chose to ask a deliberately vague question.

"I don't really know, maybe when Mr. Brockton went north. He could always keep Byron in line. The mayor dotes on her only son. He can do no wrong. You know the kind of mother that is. The kid was raised by Dr. Spock and has absolutely no sense of responsibility." Oh, dear. That's the parenting book Martha read in her search for answers, not to mention that it had been the Bible for her own mother. Was she looking into a terrible future? Would Susan and Andrew someday be caught up in a devious web of murder and intrigue?

Martha beat a hasty retreat across the sand as Wanda Wingate resumed reading, probably hoping for a fifth killing of nubile preteens.

~~~~~~~~~~~

A dreadful thought struck Martha as she pressed the button for the elevator. What if David had flushed the diaper down the
~~~~~~~~~~~

toilet? Would the helpless male idiot know the trouble that could bring? She moved to one side of the small cage to make room for a muscular man in white coveralls who carried a heavy tool kit. Was he a plumber called to fix her toilet? How embarrassing. She hoped he wouldn't get off at her floor. When he did, she hoped he wouldn't stop at her door.

He did.

Was he the angel of death in white? Her hand shook with premonition as she inserted the key. Lucas was safer in Iraq than she was in Sunny Shores. The odds of death were one in two thousand for the U.S. military over there; God knew what they were in this building. Maybe three out of every hundred.

"Ma'am," the hovering workman said, "you left this in the elevator." Martha turned and fixed her eyes on the red letters above his pocket which spelled out *Thomas Logan* in embroidered script. He handed her the rented surfboard and tipped his head in her direction. Martha watched as he walked away.

"Thank you, Mr. Logan." she called, but he didn't respond. His arms curved outward from his shoulders as if his biceps were too large for his torso, and he rolled like a sailor when he walked. She'd seen the unique swagger of the over-muscled in her gym back home. The printing on his back announced Shore Plumbing and Appliance Service. Was that tune he whistled really "Three Blind Mice?"

CHAPTER 4

The dish in 506 saw me. She looked exhausted and sunburned though, so maybe she won't remember. Now what do I do? Easy, stick to the plan. He knocked on number 501, and heard the TV snap off. A quavery male voice responded, "Who is it?"

"The plumber, Mr. Worthan. I'm here to install the water filter in your kitchen."

"I didn't order a filter." The voice climbed two levels in pitch.

"No, but the manager did. He wants to give his tenants better-tasting water." It took forever for the door to open; the man backed slowly away, his metal walker making all movement difficult.

"I'm eighty-two and never in my life have I used filtered or bottled water. What the city provides is good enough for me. I drink my ten glasses of water every day. See, here's my chart right on the refrigerator door." The plumber moved into the kitchen behind him. God, the man was slow! He wanted to knock him over and checked his impatience with great difficulty.

The old man jabbed his finger on a series of check marks on

a computer-generated chart. Indeed, the man had been careful of his health. Ten glasses of water a day. The plumber went to work, and Mr. Worthan returned to his TV.

~~~~~~~~~~~

"That should do it, Mr. Worthan." The plumber yelled his announcement through the opening between the kitchen and the dining ell. "Nothing impure will get through now." He looked around. Had he wiped away all traces of his fingerprints? Inside the fittings and out? He ran a naphtha-drenched rag over the light switch as he turned it off. The old man hobbled into the kitchen.

"You're quite the plumber. Never seen one so careful about cleaning up. You'd have made my wife proud." The plumber kept the rag in his hand to use on the doorknob when he let himself out. He'd be damn glad to get to his van and shuck out of the hot coveralls.

Great place to shop, that Goodwill store. Even if the woman in 507 remembered the name above his pocket or the name on the back, what difference did it matter? He'd never been inside Shore Plumbing and Appliance, let alone worked for them. The old guy had the TV turned back up to a screeching volume; he wouldn't live to tell any tales. It didn't take much of a push to shove these old people off into the next life. Actually, what his mother said was true: he was doing the old geezer a favor. The hall was empty as he made his way to the elevator.

~~~~~~~~~~~

When she stepped inside 507, Martha listened for the sibilant whistle of running water but didn't hear it—a good sign that her brother hadn't stuffed Susan's diaper into a reluctant plumbing system.

Instead, Horse David rocked on all fours in the middle of the living room with Andrew on his back and Susan's fat legs wrapped around his neck. He gripped her plump little feet when he bucked. Both children screamed with joy as David whinnied and snorted. She ran for her camera, happy for her children and for their uncle but also pierced by a sharp pang of loss. Lucas should be the one on all fours bringing delight to his children.

David held tight to Susan, but bucked upward to dump Andrew onto the carpet. The boy shrieked with laughter.

"Do it again," he yelled. "Do it again."

"Yes," Martha said as she returned, "Do it again. I want a picture to send to Lucas." After the photo shoot, David flattened himself onto the carpet with a bouncing Andrew still begging to be bucked off.

"Lucas is missing so much," David said.

"Yes, he is, but his college education was paid for by the army; and he knows how lucky he was. His dad and brothers will be fortunate to make half his lifetime earnings. Besides," she tapped the red, white, and blue canvas bag she carried, "we're a patriotic family. My heart goes out to those poor Iraqi people, and Lucas is proud to be their liberator."

"Right now, though, he's not making much money."

"True, and I should go back to work. I've gotten a few contracts to write for legal publishers; it doesn't pay enough but I can work at home. One good thing, the writing keeps me current on new appellate cases."

"Byron mentioned a great place for lunch. Want to try it? He recommends the hamburgers and says there's plenty of activity to keep the kids entertained."

"I'm more than ready to be amused. We've fallen into a web of crime and grief."

"Does Susan have a sunbonnet? We'll be eating outdoors."

"Don't they have umbrellas?"

"Probably. Maybe we should go early to grab one."

~~~~~~~~~~~

By eleven-thirty they sat in the shade of a large red-and-white awning sporting ads for French vermouth. They watched the incoming waves of the Atlantic, other diners, and leggy, breast-endowed waitresses in skimpy denim shorts. Andrew nibbled on pretzels while Susan carefully fisted Cheerios from her tray and worked them into her mouth. Charming dimples dotted the backs of each hand. David relaxed in the sun as he contemplated her beginning efforts toward independence. Had he looked up, he would have noticed Martha's eyes widen in surprise.

"Look toward the bar," she whispered. "Byron and the plumber. They are positively apoplectic." Their voices were loud enough to turn all heads their way. Byron stood, knocking his white plastic armchair to the floor behind him.

"You can't do that. Mine are first, and they're entirely legal." His words boomed across the patio deck; not even the whoosh of the nearby surf softened the snarling rage in his voice. "I'll see you in court." Logan whispered something to him, whereupon Byron sagged against the table. His face turned from a dark glower to pale shock. The other patrons looked uncomfortable but after a moment resumed sipping their drinks.

"He's as white as your corpses," Martha said.

"How do you know the man with him is a plumber?"

"I saw him in the hall before I came into the unit. He carried my surf board from the elevator to our door. I also read the sign on the back of his shirt. He's Thomas Logan of Shore Plumbing."

"He looks strong enough to lift that woman's body into the dumpster. I'm absolutely sure no ordinary wimp hoisted her up to the top of the trash heap."
~~~~~~~~~~~

"I'd wondered about that. How much did she weigh?"

"My guess is something between ninety and a hundred pounds."

"I do well to lift sixty-five pounds with my biceps and less with my deltoids. Most of the men at the gym double or triple that."

"Exactly. Women don't have the upper body strength men do. I think a man did it."

"You sound as if you've chosen Colonel Mustard in the parlor with a wrench."

"Do kids still play the game of Clue? That was my favorite for our family Friday night fun."

"It's still sold at Kids-R-Us. What about Byron?"

"Yeah. He might. I'd still be interesting to know if the body showed signs of being scraped or dragged across the edge of the bin."

"Can you get an autopsy report?"

"You mean would my dear and close friend, Chief Linda Elston, give it to me?" David asked.

"No, I mean could you get it through your offices in Virginia?" His grin became smug and superior, attitudes Martha knew only an older brother could display with perfection.

"It does pay to have friends here and there." he said.

"Which one of your weird friends is not a musician?" Martha asked.

"One of them is a politician, the new state senator from Elmwood Crossing. He knows how to rattle cages and bang on bars."

"It's always been my guilty dream to influence a judge for my clients," Martha said. "I wish I also had political friends."

"Influencing judicial decisions is a different matter. All I need is access to a piece of information or to have lab work expedited. Besides, didn't Stanley marry one of your fellow cheerleaders?"

"Stanley Mapes is a state senator?"

"That he is. Appointed to complete the term of Randolph Ascott. You've been too busy changing diapers to notice the uproar that appointment caused," David said. "The governor took it in the neck for naming somebody not of his own party."

"Now that's very sad."

"What? That he didn't choose from his own party?"

"No, that I didn't notice. I'll drop him a congratulatory note. Do you realize we just strung together more than a dozen complete sentences?"

"No." David looked puzzled.

"That's a post-baby record for me. Thank God for the stage and phony microphone. Andrew is enthralled with the tots dancing up there." Her son stood in front of the raised platform, apparently trying to decide if he should climb the short flight of stairs to join the other children.

"Yes, and Susan here is about to fall asleep."

"Horsey riding is blissfully fatiguing," Martha said. She smiled to herself remembering the scene she had photographed for Lucas.

The two men now leaned across their table, talking, no, more like spitting into each other's faces. Byron's wild eyes bulged and Logan looked angry enough to crush the glass he clutched in his fist. Peace had not returned to Sunny Shores. The restaurant not only provided entertainment for the children but for Martha and David as well.

The men stood, threw some bills on the table, and pounded across the wooden deck just as a waitress delivered hamburgers to Martha and David, and Chicken Tenders to Andrew.

"I wouldn't want to be facing either one of those guys," Martha said. "They're equally out of control."

"Byron's met his match," the waitress said. "Those two were on the edge of getting kicked out. Will there be anything else?"

"Catsup for Andrew, please."

"Sure enough." She produced a bottle from her apron pocket.

"What surprises me," David said, "is that they're so public about their dispute. Do you suppose they staged that outburst?"

"You do have a devious mind," Martha said. "But no, I think the rage was genuine."

"Maybe the rage was, but why show it here?" Martha helped Andrew into his chair. "There you go boy, get to work on your favorite foods." She bit into her sandwich. "This hamburger is delicious and has every accessory I could ever want." She dabbed a smear of something off of her chin. "What do you think? Is the sauce Thousand Island dressing?" David put down his hamburger and blotted his own chin.

"I find my manners deteriorating with Mia gone. I'm back to college slob housekeeping and the table manners of a wild boar."

"That we need to fix. Look around. What do you see that interests you?"

"Have you counted the belly-button rings?" David asked. "I estimate there are at least twenty. You don't see those every day in Kansas or Iowa."

"I'll do an audit, but you should watch the waitresses. They can't bend over to take orders or serve food. Do you notice that they squat down to your eye level? A girl has to keep her back straight so those low riders don't expose the complete butt."

"I hadn't noticed."

"Lucas takes it upon himself to stand behind me when I wear them. Once in the grocery store I stooped to get something off the bottom shelf and overheard an old lady snicker to her husband about my flowered briefs. I'm sure my face became as red as my underwear."

"Why do women wear such restrictive clothing?"

"Fashion, my dear brother. Fashion with a capital F. I wonder if I'd look good with a ring in my navel. Something to surprise Lucas with when he returns from the wars."

"You could also get a tattoo. There's a shop on the corner of A1A and 520. I think they're even inspected by the county health department."

"I have a tattoo that Lucas already knows about. It's a tiny rose bud. We almost named Susan for it." Martha helped Susan drink from her water glass. "Did you notice the tattoos on Byron's arms? He's a walking art gallery."

"You have to do something if you don't wear shirts," David said, "like you must decorate your belly if it's exposed."

"What do you think they were arguing about?" Martha asked.

"Sex or money,' David said. "Nothing else produces that much animosity."

"Men may kill for sex," Martha replied, "but I don't think they have shouting matches in public over obtaining that particular satisfaction."

Feeding themselves and the children held their attention for a time. When they'd finished, Martha wiped the little faces and began to gather her things while David paid the bill.

"I'll get the next meal out," she said.

"You're a stubborn woman." David happily watched Martha laugh. "I'm almost afraid to return to the condo. Who knows what we'll find today."

"Not another body, I hope." His sister picked up her daughter and walked across the wooden deck to the parking lot.

~~~~~~~~~~~

What they did find back at the condo looked very familiar to David: a rescue van, a fire truck, and three police cars in the parking lot. He found an open parking space on the street and carried the sleeping Susan to the building. They entered their fifth-floor hall in time to see an elderly person on a gurney being wheeled toward the elevator. The oxygen mask over his face made identification uncertain, but they glimpsed a gray,
~~~~~~~~~~~

hairy chest as the rescue crew passed them in the hall. The patient moaned and drew up his knees as if in abdominal pain. The gurney had come from the south end of their carpeted hallway. The image of Logan's ad-covered back heading in that direction flashed across Martha's inner vision.

"I want to go downstairs and find out what's happening," she said. "But it's the children's nap time."

"You could join the crowd of tenants we waded through downstairs," David said, "but remember what Mama always said: 'Curiosity killed the cat.'"

"That was her standard excuse for birthday and Christmas secrecy, not for dead bodies and emergency rescues."

"I'll stay with the kids." David headed for the door and opened it. "It was probably some old guy who got sick." David walked back the kitchen. "I'll have a beer while you investigate. Where are the thrillers you brought? I'm here on the beach for imaginary crimes, not real events."

"They're in the front closet in a red tote bag. If you just want to read, the kids are all yours." She was out the door before he could open his mouth. He settled them into their cribs and put himself into a chair near the balcony windows. He stared at the author's name: J.D. Robb. What could the writer possibly know about crime that he hadn't already discovered in the real world?

Fifty pages later, he rested the book on his lap and took a sip of his now-warm beer. The author did have her hooks into him, but there was entirely too much romance going on between the city detective and her rich hubby. That depressed him. Where was Martha? She should be back by now. He heard Andrew stirring in his crib. He'd best get the boy up before he yelled and woke Susan. One kid at a time was sufficient for Uncle David's skill level.

At least he'd not been the one to discover the victim they'd seen rolling out after lunch. Was there something wrong with this building? Were he and his sister in danger?

CHAPTER 5

Carolyn had the same fears as David. She'd grown up spending the summers on this beach and knew nearly every resident in the building. Mr. Worthan from 501 didn't have any family except a daughter who'd moved to Oregon. Stephanie Worthan had called, which is why Carolyn stood now beside his hospital bed. How had he been poisoned? Ricin, the doctor said; he asked if she knew how he could have gotten it.

Carolyn watched as the IV dripped nourishment into Mr. Worthan's veins. They'd pumped his stomach, used a charcoal treatment, and God knows what else. Poor man. When he opened his eyes, she reached over and patted his hand.

"Stephanie is on her way here," she said. "You're not alone." His eyes grew teary.

"She shouldn't come. It costs too much."

"Of course she should be here. You're her beloved Popsey. Mine, too, for that matter. How do you feel?"

"Terrible, but the doc says I'm lucky . . ." he swallowed and gestured toward the glass of water on his tray . . . "to be alive."

"You're one strong old goat, and I'm glad of it." Carolyn gave him a drink then reached up to brush strands of sweaty silver hair from his forehead. He smiled sweetly but must have regretted his show of pleasure; his brow instantly squeezed into the deep lines of a habitual frown.

"Aren't you supposed to be teaching those worthless hippie types over at Central Florida?" he asked.

"Another day, and they're serious anti-hippies these days. You know how it is; we're programmed to rebel against our parents. Today I'm here with you."

"Such a fuss about nothing."

"You're worth every bit of our attention. Do you have any idea how you could have been poisoned?" The old man moved his head from side to side on the white pillow before he answered.

Carolyn had done a hasty computer search. Castor beans grow everywhere and are widely known to be toxic, but ricin is a distillate from leftover mash, a byproduct of castor oil. Even so, some ambassador had been killed by an injection of it from an umbrella tip, and a less toxic form of it could reportedly be concocted in an ordinary kitchen blender.

It grows all over the U.S. and all over Iraq, where it had been tested for biological warfare potential. It is very deadly in either dry pellet, injection, or aerosol forms, and it's usually fatal if ingested.

"I eat out a lot. Do you suppose I got some spoiled clams at the Port Café last night? They go bad sometimes. The doc said something about ricin. I had rice pilaf with my fried clams."

"Ricin is made from castor beans. Sometimes kids even get sick from wearing necklaces they string together from the pretty beans. Recently prosecutors convicted an engineer on the west coast for having processed it; they suspect he meant to kill his wife. I don't know how you got it, but would you mind if I throw out everything in your kitchen? I'll try not to leave a mess. The health inspector wants to take samples first, of course."

The beans look pretty, and the eight-point leaf is beautiful. The picture she brought up in her research reminded Carolyn of the spiky-looking marijuana leaves her neighbor grew on a window sill. The neighbor thought nobody would notice. Castor bean leaves, however, shine with a lush darkness.

"Go ahead," he said. "You'll find a key in my pants pocket in the closet. I certainly know better than to go near castor beans. Those enormous leaves may look beautiful, but every gardener knows not to plant them around kids or pets." Did her dear Popsey realize that meant for certain his poisoning had been deliberate?

"Now get on along with your life," he added, "and quit worrying about me. Could you turn the TV on to CNN? Those guys put me to sleep like nothing else. I figure the world is still turning as long as they're jabbering on about it." She squeezed his hand and watched his eyelids droop. He dozed off even before she picked up the remote control.

She checked with the nurse on duty. His vital signs were fine. His color improved. They'd certainly look out for him, and yes, his daughter could see him anytime she arrived, even if it was after midnight. Carolyn wondered if she should wait here for Stephanie or get on with emptying out the apartment cupboards. Carolyn wasn't the type to wait around; her feet decided the question on their own.

~~~~~~~~~~~

It took the flustered Uncle David a full hour to change, dress, and shove food into the kids. Martha still had not returned by the time he wheeled Susan into the hallway and guided Andrew toward the elevator. They'd no doubt find her baking on the beach with her curiosity satisfied. At the last minute he decided to empty the overflowing wastebasket and take it to the dumpster.
~~~~~~~~~~~

He couldn't help smiling when he saw Carolyn's van in the parking lot. All those cheerful pictures just had to make the corners of his mouth turn up. Who needs a silver Jaguar when he could ride around inside an art gallery? He pushed Susan's stroller toward the car. The kids would enjoy the paint job. Then he noticed Carolyn standing by the open van doors. The mere sight of her caused his pulse to quicken. He felt drawn in her direction like iron shavings to a magnet, but what was she doing with all those boxes? Moving in? He hoped—hoped against his better judgment.

"Is that an art project in the making? Do you need help carrying it?"

"It is not, and yes I do. This is a save-the-elderly project. Had you met the gentleman in 501?"

"Is he the one I saw wheeled out of here earlier this afternoon?"

"The same. Mr. Worthan was poisoned. I'm throwing out everything in his kitchen as soon as the health inspector takes samples."

"Good idea." Should he help her with the stack of boxes she had balanced on her arm? "How is he doing?"

"I just came from the hospital. He feels about as well as you'd expect after losing a fight with a stomach pump. Poor man."

"How did you learn about it? Do you live here?" Now that was a dumb question. Of course he didn't care where she lived.

"His daughter, Stephanie, is a friend of mine. She lives in Oregon and teaches art at the university. She called to ask me to check on him and let him know she's on her way east." She leaned into the van for another box, giving him a good view of her cleavage.

"This is really a small town." His voice developed an adolescent squeak half way through the sentence.

"Yes, and some of us like it that way. Every new construction project adds stress to the basic systems. We're plumb out of land on this little sand bar. My mother is fighting like crazy to keep new buildings low and scarce."

"Who could disagree with that?" he asked.

"Everybody in town with a business to run, and those who've invested in beach-front property fight even harder. People who like to shop here want more business for the stores. It's been like ground zero on the city council for years."

"I'm going to the beach to find Martha. She'll take care of the kids and then I'll help you with the boxes." He had to get away from Carolyn before he broke into a sweat.

"That would be kind. I hate to throw out all of Popsey's food, but I don't want him taking any chances. There will be a lot to carry out before he comes home. Ricin is normally quite deadly, so Stephanie could be in danger as well."

"Those bodies we found—did they get the same poison?" That sounded sane enough. Was his face flushed with the effort to appear relaxed and calm?

"Linda hasn't as yet released the autopsy reports, but my guess runs in that direction." David started to wheel the baby toward the beach, but first he had to drag Andrew away from the exciting pictures. In the middle of the parking lot, a thought struck David. He stopped and turned around.

"Carolyn, when did you park in this spot?"

"Seconds ago, just before you appeared."

"Was the slot next to you empty?"

"I think so, but I didn't pay much attention."

"Martha must have gone somewhere. Strange she didn't let me know."

"Maybe she's hiding from her children. Moms do get tired of responsibility, you know."

"You're probably right, but it's not like my sister to slip off without saying anything." Slip. It wasn't hard to picture Carolyn in a lacy slip, though he doubted she had one on under her denim mini skirt. Very nice legs. He dragged his eyes away.

"The members of one's family often provide the worst surprises. Mine always do." Carolyn laughed and pointed toward the front of his pants. My God! Was he bulging like an aroused teenager?

"Do you realize your cell phone is ringing?" she asked. David felt blood rush to his face as he pulled the instrument from his belt.

"This is David," he said then paused.

"You did what? . . . Where are you?" When David pushed the end button, he turned to Carolyn.

"Is there any chance you could help me return these babies to their lawful mother? My sister is down the road on a mysterious stake-out, and I am fresh out of wheels."

"You're a lucky man. I just happen to have a car seat that will fit Andrew. You ride in the back and hold the baby. Make sure she faces you and I'll drive with excruciating care." She buckled Andrew in. David noticed that the cloth upholstery was worn through in places and stained in others, but the engine had a deep-throated roar. Carolyn asked her one and only question.

"Which way?"

"South. Some taco place near the air base." She pulled onto the highway with a surprising burst of power. A few minutes later David spotted his rental car on the ocean side of the highway.

"That's it," he said. "Drive on past until we're out of sight, then turn around."

"Am I doing anything illegal?" she asked, "because I certainly hope so."

"Not yet," he replied. "That comes later."

~~~~~~~~~~~

The sooty ambiance of the smoke-stained pine walls, worn
~~~~~~~~~~~

terra cotta floor, bull fight posters, and wooden booths of Teresa's Tacos subdued both David and Carolyn. Andrew, by contrast, began to bounce in his uncle's arms and clap his hands as soon as they were inside. David hustled the party into an empty booth, but not before Susan spied her mother and shrieked.

With an involuntary gasp and knee-jerk movement toward Susan's screams, Martha gave herself away. She slid from her bar stool and hurried over to claim her baby.

"I thought you would be more discrete," she hissed at her brother. "You've blown my cover."

"Exactly," David said. Martha glowered, but took the howling baby into her arms.

"So much for being surreptitious," she whispered as she patted Susan.

Thomas Logan walked toward them. He wore a leather vest which completely bared his impressively muscled arms and the assortment of blue and red tattoos adorning them. A leather string corralled his wispy pony tail, and a suspicious scowl creased his very large, very round face. He threw Martha a small salute as he walked past and glared at Carolyn. They watched through the front windows as he mounted a gleaming Harley hog and roared off into the evening traffic.

"The deal here is, you place your order at the counter, pay for it then, and wait for your name to be called." Carolyn said. "Best Tex-Mex food anywhere, but you serve your own meals."

"Teresa's would go over big in Elmwood Crossings," Martha said. "We could even park a Harley-Davidson set out front to create a dangerous aura." David took the few steps to the order counter and returned with menus, chips, and fresh salsa.

"The kids have been fed," he said. "Would Andrew like a coke?" Martha scanned the plastic-covered menu.

"Number 5 for me, bonuelos for Andrew, and nothing for Susan."

"I'll have the Chilli Rellenos," Carolyn said, "and a

Marguerita." David placed their orders and received a double ring on the dinner bell plus an "Olé" for his tip.

~~~~~~~~~~~

"We can't talk here," he announced between chews, "but I'll be interested to find out what you're up to." He wore the expression of a nasty seventh-grade teacher who'd just been hit in the back of the head by a blow-gun missile. Carolyn looked from Martha to David and back again.

"You two could be opposing armies. Fight-to-the-death is written across your faces."

"That's the way it's always been," Martha said, "ever since he used my birthday Barbie Doll to test his red-bandana parachute from the top of our grandpa's silo."

"Then what brings the two of you together in Sunny Shores?"

"My brother is recovering from a broken heart," Martha said, "and I thought the kids would cheer him up."

"My sister needs help with the children while her husband is overseas," David said.

"I see," Carolyn said. "It's very clear that you two hate each other. I have but one question for you, Martha. Why were you at the bar flirting with the owner of a pawn shop? Getting ready to turn David in for cash?"

"Pawn shop? I thought he was a plumber." Martha's eyes widened with surprise.

"Him? He's never done an honest day's work in his life. He wouldn't be caught dead soiling his hands, let alone digging into sewers. In high school he had greasy hair, plenteous acne, and too many rings worn in too many places. Be careful, he's run through more wives than Henry the Eighth. For some reason, they just don't stick around."

The party nibbled tortilla chips in silence, waiting for their
~~~~~~~~~~~

food. It was hard to find small talk with each of them wondering what Martha had been up to and Martha herself filled with resentment about the abrupt interference with her pursuit. Carolyn entertained herself trying to teach pat-a-cake to Susan. When the baby didn't respond, she turned to Andrew.

"Andrew, as big brother, it's your job in life to be a good leader. Susan will copy whatever you do, so let's show her how to pat-a-cake. I know you're too old for the game, but please give her a little demonstration." Andrew nodded soberly, but he soon got into the spirit and dissolved into happy shrieks and giggles. Nobody was surprised when Susan began to follow the motions with her own two hands. Martha beamed.

"You're a pro, Carolyn," she said.

"Long years spent working as a camp counselor. I'm an endless resource for silliness."

"Pawn shop," David said when they tired of watching the children play. "It's odd that we have a loan shark and a pawnbroker hovering over the scene of three murders."

"It's all financial, just like Lucas said," Martha replied. "Follow the money."

"Speaking of money," Carolyn said, "I'm wondering if I could get Teresa to hang some of my acrylics here. I do have a good collection of beach scenes. They might sell and would certainly improve the decor."

"I'd buy one," Martha said. "It would be a perfect souvenir from Sunny Shores. On second thought, what price range are we in?"

"Don't I wish I could ask thousands for my work," Carolyn said. "Even four would be nice. I'll bring a few over for you to look at. You might want to think about a small, framed water color that I don't prize above my life."

"The way you're going, Martha, you won't need a souvenir; you'll have scars to remember Florida. I'm wondering if you'll get out of the state alive." David's acid tones reeked of disapproval. "David!" was called before Martha could retort, and he soon delivered extremely hot plates of food to their table.

~~~~~~~~~~~

"I'm sticking with you until I find out what Martha is up to," Carolyn said.

They'd finished eating and walked outside. "You're much too interesting. Perhaps I should take Andrew for a hostage."

"Nobody from Iowa is interesting," David said. "You'll only get bored hanging around us."

"Hah! I'll be right behind you," Caroline said, "and don't try to outrun me. This old thing has more oomph than you think."

"It looks to me as if it doesn't know its front from its back," Martha said. "I've never seen such a going-both-ways design."

"I believe the original engine has been replaced," David said.

"You're both right. Besides it's utterly charming exterior modifications, it's had a heart transplant. I had a mechanic look at the engine, which turns out to belong in a Porsche. The poor fellow couldn't figure out how it had been installed, let alone why it works."

"Okay. You win," David said. "We'll drive sedately back to the condo."

"Who put you in charge of how we'll drive?" Martha asked. "Don't forget I have the keys." She dangled them in front of his face. "You're to manage the kids and the car seats. Now hop to it!" David groaned.

"You two need a mother," Carolyn said, "and I have half a notion to lend you mine."

The sun began its descent toward the horizon as they drove north on the palm-lined highway. Orange light and purple clouds dominated the western sky in a breathtaking display. David patted Susan's arm from his location in the rear,
~~~~~~~~~~~

squeezed between his niece and nephew. Martha sang some silly kid's song at the top of her lungs as she drove, and Andrew squeaked along, pounding merrily on the protective bar of his car seat. Susan's eyelids began to droop toward her fat, round cheeks.

This was what he'd come to Florida for: beauty, peace, and connection to his family. He felt a deep kind of satisfaction that had eluded him entirely since Mia walked out. Trust your instincts, he heard his mother say. Listen to the Holy Spirit. Did this feeling of joy come from the beautiful surroundings or was it a gift of grace. What did Carolyn have to do with his happiness?

Nothing! The last thing he needed was a cross-country romance.

Meditating on his peaceful state, he didn't see the single headlight emerge from the right side of the highway. The roar of the Harley he couldn't miss. The damn fool was going to ram them from the side. He flung one arm in front of Andrew and threw himself across the baby as Martha swerved into the left lane. The hog roared off ahead of them, probably doing seventy in a residential zone.

Carolyn turned into the parking lot behind them and stormed over to their car. "That damn fool! I hope his license is up for renewal. I'll sic Linda on him. What an ass!" Carolyn's beauty took on a special glow when she was angry, but David chided himself for noticing.

"Martha, what did you say to him back at that bar?" David asked.

"I suppose he thinks I was playing with him," she said, "you know, being a tease."

"That happened to him all the time in high school. I'm afraid we played some very cruel games. We'd encourage him, take the presents he brought from his dad's pawn shop, then dump him immediately. It was never pretty."

"I didn't learn to fake disinterest when girls did that sort of stuff to me."

"Is that why you're an FBI agent? So you could be certifiably superior with a badge to prove it?"

"Probably. But I also love the gadgets."

"Let's get the kids inside where they'll be safe," Martha said.

"I'm not going away until you let me in on your plans," Carolyn said. "Besides, David promised to help me carry in these boxes. I hope the health inspector has been here and gone."

CHAPTER 6

Martha and David followed Carolyn into Unit 501. A copy of the health inspection report lay on the kitchen counter. The techs had taken samples of absolutely everything in the kitchen, from salt to pepper, milk to molasses, and Cole slaw to corn flakes. A note scrawled across the bottom advised Carolyn not to throw food out until the lab had completed their analysis.

"At least I'm not hungry, but I hate to leave this stuff here. What if Stephanie eats something? She could be poisoned."

"Stephanie can have breakfast with us," Martha said. "I'll do pancakes and sausage links since that's Andrew's favorite menu."

"That's very kind of you. There's no food in my dad's unit. He cleans the place out before he heads north because he doesn't want a condo crawling with ants and cockroaches when he returns."

"Well then, you should eat with us as well." If Martha noticed the horrified expression on David's face, she was smart enough to say nothing.

"Thank you," Carolyn said. "Can I come sweaty? I treasure my early run on the beach."

"Come anyway you like. I'll be the one watching and waving from the balcony while you two idiots pound your knees to a pulp."

Thursday, July 10th

After breakfast, Stephanie headed for the hospital. The other three sipped coffee on the balcony.

"Carolyn," Martha asked, "I've looked in the phone book. I can't find a pawn shop owned by a Thomas Logan." Carolyn's stunned look turned to puzzlement as she tried to digest the question.

"Thomas Logan? Who is that?"

"The man I followed to Teresa's last night."

Carolyn set her mug down and shook her head.

"No. That was Sly Fately. Always was and always will be. I've never heard of a Thomas Logan."

"But he wore the uniform with the printing on it: Thomas Logan, Shore Plumbing and Appliance. I can see the letters before my eyes this very minute." David leaned over the balcony to watch the half-dozen surfers glide to shore.

"When did you see him in the uniform?" Carolyn asked.

"Yesterday morning after I surfed. We rode the elevator together up to this floor. He carried my surf board to my door then walked on toward the end of the hall."

"Did he go into 501?" David asked, suddenly paying attention.

"I don't know. That direction. Could be. That's why I followed him. I was trying to find out."

"Martha, if he poisoned Mr. Worthan, you need to stay away from him," David said. There was no missing the emphatic voice of authority.

"I agree," Carolyn said. "There's nothing good about him. Stephanie would concur as well."

"All I want to do is visit his shop." They didn't need to gang up on her this way.

"No way, Martha. I'm not letting you out of my sight."

"David, it's a business," Martha said. "I promise I won't enter the door unless there are other customers inside." He was doing it again, acting like the big brother. "You and I are both adults now, in case you hadn't noticed."

"Another customer won't offer protection if the nut decides to pull a gun from under the counter and shoot you. Your kids need a live mother."

"He's not that sort," Martha protested. "I know him better than you do."

"Yeah. Ten minutes sitting beside him on a bar stool qualifies you to complete his entire psychological profile. Wonderful! We need you in Washington to save the nation from terrorists." Both Martha and David had gotten very red in the face.

"I hate it when you get sarcastic," Martha said. "You can outtalk me any day, but you cannot change my mind."

"We can all go," Carolyn interrupted. "I shop used furniture stores for picture frames. That would give me a good excuse."

"Just exactly what would we do once inside the store? Buy jewelry? And what would we do with the kids? Do you want them in the line of fire?" David floundered in the rip tide of feminine persuasion.

"You've spent too much of your life around crooks," Martha said. "He's just a harmless home-boy surfer."

"Then why did you follow him?"

"We could always blame it on my whacky hormones. I'm lacking certain satisfactions with Lucas off in Iraq."

"That's slightly better than the insanity defense. Even so, surfing with sharks would be safer."

"Yes," Carolyn said, "but Sly would never be attractive no matter how jumpy your hormones are." David wished they'd get off the subject of sex.

~~~~~~~~~~~

Inside the pawnshop, Carolyn walked directly toward a stack of framed posters lined up against the back wall while David and Martha inspected baby furniture. Sly busied himself unlocking a glass-top jewelry cabinet for a customer. When the customer left, he headed for Carolyn.

"Carol baby! What brings you here? You want to pawn your wedding ring?"

"Do these look like something I'd wear on my finger?" She pointed to a stack of frames she'd lined up against the stereo cabinets. "How much?"

"For you, half price. Look on the backs." He helped her carry her choices to the sales counter and rang up her purchases.

"Who are those people you brought in? New in-laws?"

"You know I'm not married. Drop it, Sly."

"Yeah, I know." He smirked. "And how is your son?"

"Beautiful, smart, talented, and good," Caroline said. She worked hard to keep her voice modulated and cool. "That's how he is."

"No need to get nasty," Sly smirked. "You're no better than me now."

"You must have married every slut in our class. Who is it this time?" Carolyn pointed to his wedding ring.

"I just wear this to keep the babes away. What they love best is the ring of this cash register." He punched a button to produce the proper sound. "I'm sorry it didn't work out for you with that professor. What a jerk!"

"He's not the only man in this world," Carolyn said.

Sly responded with a snort and turned toward David and Martha. "Could I help you with something? I have other cribs in the back if you don't like these."

"Actually," Martha said, "We're shopping for a gun,
~~~~~~~~~~~

something small that I can carry in my purse. I'd also like some pepper spray." She smiled at him sweetly, with all the open innocence of an Iowa sunflower.

"Right over here, Mamie. Everything from derringer to Uzi. Take your pick. Of course I'll have to do a background check, and you might not like that."

"Mamie?" David whispered. "Our mother will be shocked. It's very uncreative."

"I had a purse with a big *M* on the front. What was I to do? Besides, you know how much we loved the cookies Great Aunt Mamie baked."

"I forbid the gun," he said. "You'll end up shooting yourself or one of the kids."

"How else can I get his fingerprints?" Martha whispered. She strode over to the gun display. "That one looks perfect," she pointed.

"Nice choice." Sly stooped to unlock the cabinet. "Five hundred dollars and three days," he said. "Want me to box it for you?" He hadn't yet touched its shiny surface.

"Would you show me how to hold it?" Martha asked.

"We don't need ammunition." Carolyn said, peering over Martha's shoulder. "It's a prop for a picture I'm doing on commission. A poster."

Damn! David found himself nodding with approval.

Sly took a handkerchief from his pocket and picked the pistol up with it. He laid it on a black velvet pad on the counter.

"Nice piece, so I keep it clean. Owned by a wealthy couple. I'm not sure who shot whom first. Let me see your driver's license. Lessons you get elsewhere. There's a range over on the west side of the Banana River south of 520. I'll need a hundred dollar deposit." Martha wrote out a check and handed it over. He shoved it into a drawer and handed her a form. While she filled in the blanks, he carried Carolyn's collection of pictures to the conch car. David was certain Carolyn exaggerated the swing of her hips as she walked out ahead of Sly.

"Martha, you don't need to go through with this," David said. "His prints are all over Carolyn's frames."

"I can't stop now. It would give me away as a fraud. Besides, it's such a pretty gun and I always wanted to learn to shoot."

"You are the fraud." David strode angrily out the door and stood where he could watch both Carolyn and Sly. They put the posters into the van, and Sly kept his hands to himself. Martha followed him out and got into the rental Buick.

"I'm going to the hospital," Carolyn said, starting the engine.

"And I'm off for some shopping," Martha announced. Both women drove off, leaving David standing on the curb with a child attached to each arm.

~~~~~~~~~~~

In the time it took Martha to circle the block and return, David counted to four hundred. At around two hundred, Andrew tugged at his arm and pointed to a frozen yogurt shop across the street. The meaning of the wooden cone on the sandwich board in front could be grasped by anyone over the age of eighteen months.

"Sorry," Martha shouted through her rolled-down window. "I got carried away with the chance to solve a crime. Don't be so smug. You get to do it all the time."

"I know, and you're home polishing the kitchen floor to a perfect shine while I have my fun. May I suggest you get back to your career when you reach Elmwood Crossing? Get a life, as the disrespectful young now say."

"Not to mention, 'get money.' My idea of shopping won't work without it. Hop in and don't be a sorehead."

"Can't do. Andrew has spotted a treasure and we're off on the hunt." Martha followed the line of her son's extended arm and nodded.

"That I might be able to afford."
~~~~~~~~~~~

Carolyn waved as she drove past. She must have circled the block as well, just to see what her new friends were up to. Would a frozen dessert chill his interest in this beautiful woman? Probably not.

"Even her name is fortunate," Martha said as she locked the car. "I can see entwined C and D embroidered in subdued ivory thread on creamy bed linens. Yes. I think I'll order a set and start working on the design. Carolyn and David fit together in perfect alphabetical order. May you acquire many little CDs."

David carried Susan and raced Andrew across the street as soon as the lighted traffic man gave his approval. Andrew homed in on the wooden ice cream cone ahead with Martha hustling after him. David selected a spot beside the window overlooking the street. He led Andrew to the counter while Martha settled Susan into a small chair that hung conveniently from the end of the table.

"I'll have a chocolate sundae," she told David, "with sprinkles on top. Are you treating?"

"I am, and what'll it be for you, Mr. Andrew?" The boy, suddenly shy, whispered into his uncle's ear.

"One chocolate sundae, one chocolate cone, and one peanut-butter shake," David ordered.

They had nearly finished their frozen treats when Martha's eyes widened and her spine straightened.

"Wanda Wingate just went into Sly's store."

"Who?"

"My baby-sitter. She's certainly not emaciated, so what is she doing in a pawn shop?"

"It's none of our business."

"It might be. That looks like our TV Sly is carrying into his store." David's head jerked around to look.

"Couldn't be. Come on. Mop up your chocolate-covered baby, and let's get out of here before you come up with any other bad ideas." David dabbed a bunch of paper napkins into the water glass and wiped his nephew's fingers and face. The sticky T-shirt would have to wait for a laundry day. Martha drove north in silence.

~~~~~~~~~~~

"See. Not to worry. It's still here." David turned the TV on and watched a soap-opera couple kissing. Did everything in life have to remind him of what he needed and didn't have? Martha sighed.

"Well, it was a TV set just like this one, and it was Wanda."

"TV's all look pretty much alike these days. I'm sure you're wrong." The phone rang and Martha picked it up, listening while she jiggled Susan on one hip. David heard a long series of uh-huh's before she hung up.

"Would you please go down to 501? Carolyn wants us both but I have to stay here to put the kids down for their naps."

"Don't you want to go? I could watch your children."

"Get out of here. I don't know a thing about finger prints or fiber clues."

"If you're talking about a crime, it's a matter for the local police."

"Carolyn doesn't want to get her sister involved. Something about bad publicity. Shoo! Go!" Susan began to root around on her mother's breast. "See, she wants to nurse, and you're not the least bit qualified."

"I'm on vacation," David said. "No crime for two weeks. I need a break."

"I wish I already had that gun. I could wave it around and make you pay attention."

David went to Unit 501, where the dust-free rectangle on top of a mahogany stand told its own story. Carolyn and Stephanie stood in the middle of the living room.
~~~~~~~~~~~

"I told her not to touch a thing," Carolyn said. David eyed the blondes. Do they bloom eternally in Florida like the oleanders? Forget oleanders—they're poisonous. Think beach daisies or blue hydrangeas. Think diversion.

"How is your father doing?" he asked.

"He's better," Stephanie said, "and anxious to get back home. We came to get his clothes and found this." She waved her hand toward the empty TV stand. "I don't know if anything else is missing."

"You didn't turn the lights on? Didn't open the blinds?" David asked. They shook their heads.

"Wonderful. Now call the police." They shook their heads.

"Why not?" How could he get them to do the sensible thing?

"It had to be taken by someone in this building. We'll just get it back and let that be the end of it. These poor people have suffered enough."

"I'm afraid I know just where it is," David said. "Let's go see Mr. Sly Poltron." He started toward the door. "Do you have any documentation on the TV? Maybe the serial number?" Stephanie moved toward the empty stand.

"Be careful. Don't touch any surfaces." Stephanie nodded and went toward the front hall closet.

"Dad might have some plastic gloves in here with the cleaning supplies, although he hires that work done." David held the knobs by the edges to open the doors to the closet and stood back for Stephanie to look. "How do I get them without touching anything?" she asked.

"I doubt you'd be a suspect. We know where you were, so touch as little as possible." She pulled a pair of thin plastic gloves from a box and put them on.

"I think he keeps the papers under the TV. There's a little drawer in the cabinet. Should I look?"

"Better not." David inspected his watch. "I saw a TV go into the front of Sly's pawn shop half an hour ago. It might be leaving out the back as we speak. Hot stuff doesn't sit long near the source of the article. You can look around for other items when we get there. You know your dad's jewelry, don't you?" Stephanie nodded.

"That I do. All he has is a Rolex and a wedding ring, which I believe are with him. My grandmother's better pieces are in a safe deposit box at the bank."

"What about this stack of mail?" David pointed to a pile on the table near the front door. "Did either of you bring it in?" Carolyn shook her head, and David found himself mesmerized by the swing of the golden hair against her shoulders.

"The mail was here when we arrived," Stephanie said.

"Better watch his credit records closely for the next few weeks and months. Stealing credit cards can be quite profitable."

"I read that some woman near Orlando got away with nearly $300,000 in three years by stealing credit promotions," Stephanie said. "She worked in a campus mail room and used cards the students didn't know they'd received."

"You got it. That kind of theft is easy to do and hard to stop."

"It's those damn balconies," Stephanie said. "There never was any trouble here until they had to be replaced."

"That you can explain to me later. For now, let's head for Sly's. I must be crazy to do this without the locals. Actually, my brain seems to quit working when I'm around beautiful women. The two of you do me in completely."

"Are you accusing us of theft of mental powers?" Carolyn asked. David concentrated. He tried to imagine her as bald and fat.

"You could shave your head and put on about fifty pounds." Please, he thought, though I don't think it would help. She'd look Rubenesque and sexy as hell. That was a bad choice of images. She now lolled seductively on a paisley-covered day bed, entirely nude and satisfied, her head wrapped in a turban.

He nearly forgot to use his handkerchief when he closed the door to the unit.

"Should I lock it?" Stephanie asked. "I hate to touch anything."

"Didn't you bring the keys with you?"

"Yes, but Dad said Wanda also had a key."

"Then her fingerprints will be justifiably all over this place. Let's try to catch the TV before it runs away." His next thoughts were even more troublesome than the Ruben nude. Did he know a gallery owner in Kansas City he could bribe to do a show of Carolyn's art? Of course not. He didn't want her anywhere near Kansas City.

Just when in life do we learn to keep a straight face while our thoughts rage in forbidden territory? In kindergarten, he realized, after the first day when your mother asks you what happened at school. That must be when we start to have private thoughts along with the desire to keep them to ourselves.

How would he make it up to Martha that he wasn't taking her along to the pawn shop? It would bring rancor to Thanksgiving and Christmas dinners for the rest of his natural life. But he had to hurry. The truck could be loaded and leaving at this very minute.

"I'll drive. You look too edgy," Carolyn said.

"I am nervous. I'm cutting through Bureau rules and regs like a chain saw. I wouldn't do this for just anybody. Aren't there any ugly women in Florida?" Both women smiled and patted his arm.

"There, there," Stephanie said. "Carolyn did say you were very nice."

"You kept the keys, didn't you? We don't want anyone going into your father's unit while we're gone."

"There, there," she said again and jangled a set in front of his face. "Calm down."

"I'm used to doing these things after endless hours of planning, with skilled, trained fellow agents."

"We're trained. Absolutely," Stephanie said.

"We're excellent observers," Carolyn added. "There's nothing like an artist to notice all the details. You do the strong-arm stuff; we'll be your best eyes ever."

"And ears," Stephanie said. "Don't forget we listen."

"A skill we honed standing outside the principal's office with our ears pressed to the door while he fooled around with the guidance counselor."

"Why do I think I've come to an important Y in my life and taken the wrong fork?" David asked. During the few minutes it took to reach the center of town, he pondered his own question.

"Pull around to the back of the building. You two go in the front door and keep Sly busy. I'll check for a rear exit." Carolyn parked her conch car behind a large white enclosed truck that had backed up to the loading platform.

There was indeed a TV sitting on the dock. David wrote down the serial number, wishing he had the papers now stored in Stephanie's purse. He turned toward a sudden noise and faced a very thick and hairy pair of calves.

"What the hell are you doing here? This is private property, and you are trespassing," Sly shouted. The two long-legged, bare-shouldered blondes stood behind him rolling their eyeballs.

"You are probably correct, but we're looking for a certain missing set. Stephanie, would you read the serial number of your father's TV? And Sly, would you see if the numbers on this plate are the same? Perhaps we've found a match." Sly looked from David to the very muscular workman in coveralls who had appeared behind the women. 'Superior Trucking,' it said on the man's pocket.

"Sorry Stephanie," Sly said. "It's not your dad's missing TV. A woman brought this in saying it was hers. Now go back up to the front of the store where you belong." Stephanie began to read aloud as David checked his note.

"In that case, you're dealing in stolen merchandise," David said. "Not a particularly good activity for the owner of a pawn shop."

"Take that damn set and get out of here," Sly yelled. The trucker stooped to lift the TV.

"No! Not you!" Sly pointed to David. "You! I don't do stolen goods. I've been had."

"Before we touch it, I'd like to call the police to get it dusted for fingerprints. It's evidence of a crime." What was Carolyn doing kneeling on the floor behind Sly?

"You got your damn TV, so leave." Sly was now in the yelling mode. He squatted and prepared to push the TV off the platform. He jerked to a stop and they all turned toward the squeal of brakes in the alley behind them.

"Hi, Linda," Carolyn yelled. "You're just in time."

"How in the hell . . . ?" Sly asked. His normally florid complexion paled.

"I saw this little wire," Carolyn said, "and I just happened to have scissors in my purse. We're only a block from the station. Have you had many thefts lately, Linda?"

"Not really. We usually don't find out about them until the owners get back in October."

"Stephanie and I regret making trouble for you. We tried to keep the problem quiet." The trucker had begun to move toward the door into the store.

"I can't stay out here," Sly said. "God knows what is happening inside."

"There are two policewomen guarding your stock. It will take forever to do a thorough inventory, so you'll be closed for at least a month."

A car pulled up behind the police cruisers. Martha hopped out. Her lips were clamped so tightly shut you'd think she'd been chewing super glue. She glared at David.

"Where are the kids?" he asked. A good offense always tops a defense.

"I left them with Mrs. Wingate."

"We'd best be getting back. It looks like she stole this TV from 501."

"TV maybe, but I doubt she'll steal the kids."

"I forgot. You're an expert at character analysis."

"I've worked with more crooks than you have."

"Yeah, but you're supposed to believe them. I'm not." Carolyn frowned at both of them and shook her head.

"Linda, could you send a team over to unit 501 to investigate the theft of Mr. Worthan's TV? We've found it here, and we're pretty sure who took it."

"Can't you get any work out of this worse-than-useless federal agent? My staff will be busy for days checking the inventory against stolen items; it's something I've been itching for an excuse to do."

"That might be a waste of time," David said. "Anything he thinks was stolen would be gone to wherever this TV was headed. Our trucker here might know that destination. It's probably in another state."

But there was no trucker on the platform or anywhere near it.

"You're so smart!" Chief Linda said. "Where is your phantom trucker?"

"His truck is solid enough," Carolyn said. David felt good about her coming to his defense; then he regretted it. "He wouldn't go off without his truck," she added.

"That's my truck," Sly said. "It was a customer who followed me out of the store. Never seen him before in my life." In spite of the trouble he was in, Sly looked extremely pleased with himself.

~~~~~~~~~~

That evening, Martha and David sat on their balcony watching the daylight fade and the lights from the fishing pier
~~~~~~~~~~

to the north begin their nightly glow. "I don't for one minute believe Mr. Worthan asked Wanda to pawn his TV set," Martha said. "Even Stephanie admitted he watches the news all day long."

"If it had been pawned, it wouldn't have left the store."

"Sly explained that." Martha sipped some of the sweet wine Carolyn had brought for dinner two nights earlier. "Sly said he took it out on the dock to blow dust from the interior and had no intention of loading it onto his truck."

"Anyway, the net result is zilch."

"Right. We're no closer to finding out who killed Agnes and those other ladies than we were this morning."

"Or who poisoned Mr. Worthan," David added.

"You don't suppose he did the killing himself," Martha asked, "and accidently ingested some of the stuff."

"Hell of a thing to get careless about. Besides, he's not strong enough to drag a body to the dumpster, let alone lift it in."

"I had no idea a vacation on Sunny Shores would be so interesting," Martha said, "and we haven't been to a single theme park in Orlando."

"Taking the kids to the playground in the city park was a good idea," David said. "They fell asleep tonight like they'd been drugged."

"Drugged they were—sedated by the swings and slides."

"I don't think Mrs. Wingate will baby-sit them again. She wasn't happy about being accused of stealing Mr. Worthan's TV." David picked up the binoculars.

"She's lucky Mr. Worthan wanted to protect his long-time neighbor. What are you looking at?"

"It might be a group of dolphins. Want to see?" He handed over the glasses.

"You're right," Martha said. "I see thin straight tail fins breaking the surface. How still it is tonight!"

"Viewing such tranquility," David said. "It's hard to believe there are real problems all around us."

"Do you remember back in the 1980s, when so many of the Iowa farmers went crashing down because of debt overload?" Martha asked.

"Vaguely. It didn't affect us much, but we had friends in school wearing worried frowns and last year's faded clothes."

"Nothing on our rural landscape revealed the turmoil in the farmers' financial lives," Martha said.

"I sneaked out of school once and went to a farm sale," David said. "They sold everything. No way could the farmer stay in business."

"Dad said it was credit that did them in. Too many bank loans and no way to repay."

"You're suggesting something similar happened here."

"Not just here. According to Wanda, every condominium along the beach is in the same situation. All the balconies succumbed to salt spray. Byron's loan business must be booming."

"It makes me wonder," David said, "if we should be sitting out here."

"I think the original decks have already been replaced."

"Let's hope so. I'd not want to end up five stories down, even if the beach is made of sand."

CHAPTER 7

A knock on the door interrupted their discussion about defective balconies.

"That must be Carolyn and Stephanie. They said they'd stop by after they got Mr. Worthan settled in." When David opened the door to admit them, Stephanie held up two bottles.

"Dad said to give you these. He's grateful that you brought back his TV."

"Has he changed his story?"

"Not yet. Just changed his mind. He can't sleep without his shot of CNN."

"Some night cap." David motioned his guests inside.

"We brought a better one." Carolyn held up a glass pitcher and a can of frozen lemonade. "Simple, quick, and excellent. A trick my mother taught me—the poor man's whiskey sour. Is there a blender in your kitchen?"

"I think so." Martha and Carolyn began to search the cupboards as Stephanie and David went out to the balcony.

"You said you'd fill me in about these little porches," David said. She waved toward the sliding glass doors and the ocean.

"Things don't last forever here in the salty air. Silverware, wallpaper, and porches all give in to the humid peculiarities of the seaside. Little cracks form in the concrete floors. Salt gets into the openings and eats away the steel reinforcing rods; after about twenty years, the floor is unsafe. Replacement costs like hell, so people living on fixed incomes can't pay their assessments, which in some cases amount to sixty thousand dollars."

"Add to that the recent drop in portfolio values and investment income, and you have monetary disaster," Carolyn added. She carried a tray of frothy drinks to the porch. "Try this."

"Thank you," David said. Carolyn sank into the chair opposite him and watched his reaction to her concoction.

"Some of the tenants sold out and moved in with their children up north. That's where the board thought the woman in the dumpster had gone."

"Apparently she first willed it to her daughter," Carolyn said.

"But now Byron holds a quitclaim deed," Stephanie said.

"Well anyway, cheers!" Martha said, lifting her glass. "It doesn't seem like an appropriate toast in the midst of this talk of dire need, but the world keeps spinning."

"It does for those of us with jobs and income," Stephanie said.

"I find it hard to dredge up sympathy for anybody who owns this ocean view," Martha said. "It seems like the height of luxury."

"Things are rarely what they seem."

"So who owns this condo?" David asked.

"We don't know. It's the one in dispute."

"That woman you found in the dumpster lived here?" Martha's voice rose as the shock took hold. "I'm using her towels and her kitchen?"

"Afraid so. Byron rented it out to get income to make the payments."

"Then we're not legally occupying the space at all," Martha said.

"Who would kick you out? Certainly not Byron. Certainly not another tenant who wants to see the fees paid. Certainly not the officers of the court. They're forty-five minutes away on the other side of the county and wouldn't know you're here."

"I feel as if the floor was falling out from under me," Martha said.

"Not a good image," Carolyn said, "but it could happen."

"Why do you say that?" David asked. "Good stuff!" he added, raising his glass to Carolyn.

"I have my suspicions about the company that repaired the balconies," Carolyn said. "I noticed about as many new steel bars on their truck at the end of the days they worked here as at the beginning."

"Who have you told about that?"

"My mother, my sister, Byron. Nobody wants to dig up the floors to find out what's in them, and nobody else paid attention during the repair work. I told you. We artists are trained to observe carefully."

"Correction. Dad watched," Stephanie said. "He's a retired civil engineer, so he deliberately moved his chair to the patio doors and observed every bit of the work as it was being done. He's sure there are the required re-bars on his balcony."

"You're certain he didn't nod off watching the news?" Carolyn asked.

"I'm sure. He doesn't miss a thing. Don't forget, I was once a teenager under his control. I know him very well."

"Pretty good recommendation," David said.

"So, until a balcony falls, there's no way to go after the repair company," Martha said.

"My suspicions could be so much hooey," Carolyn said, "which is what Byron claims."

"What does he care? His unit's on the ground floor,"

"He wouldn't like the one above to fall on his head."

"Most people don't use their balconies. They stay inside with the AC turned on full blast," Stephanie said.

"And all the balcony furniture is light plastic."

"Exactly."

"What do you know about the lab report on your dad's kitchen, Stephanie," David asked.

"Completely negative. We didn't need to throw out anything. Dad thinks he got some bad clams."

"Ricin doesn't form in clams by accidental spoilage."

"I know, but he doesn't want to think badly of anyone, especially not of Wanda, his very helpful neighbor."

"How about the water," Martha asked. "Is it good?" Stephanie examined the lab report.

"It checked out fine."

"I'd get bottled water for him if I were you."

"I agree. I picked up a twenty-four pack this afternoon. The problem is in getting him to drink it, and I'm sure he'll refill the ones he does use from the tap."

"Sly was doing something in an apartment down your dad's way," Martha said. "I wish I'd paid attention to which one."

"How did Mr. Worthan get the ricin if it wasn't in his food or water?"

"Did they examine his medications?"

"I'll find out," Stephanie said.

"Let's go through the kitchen again, and check each item in the cupboards against this list. Maybe they missed something."

"Also, did he have breakfast with anyone? His food could have been tampered with at a restaurant."

"I'm still betting on the plumber in the kitchen with a wrench," Martha said. David laughed.

"I'll find out if he ate any meals out that day," Stephanie said.

"And I'll sit here and read my mystery."

The three women sniffed their disapproval as they left.

"Your brother is determined not to be helpful," Carolyn whispered, "but I want whoever killed Agnes to pay for the crime. She was a world-class good person." They tiptoed into the kitchen in order not to waken Mr. Worthan, who snoozed on the living room sofa. The sound of the TV covered their conversation.

"Actually, my brother can't resist crime. He'd like to stand back and do nothing, but he also wants to solve the mystery."

"I have to know my dad is safe here before I head back to Oregon," Stephanie said. "A friend is covering my classes, but I can't expect that kind of help for long. He has his own work to do."

"What's our system?" Martha asked.

"Everything out of the cupboards and onto the counters," Carolyn said. "We put each item back when we've checked it against the list. Anything left on the counter was missed by the lab techs." The three women set to work.

"One thing nice, his cabinets will be super clean when we're finished." Stephanie pulled a cleaning spray and rags from the hall closet. "I'll wipe them out and spray with ant poison before we put the food back."

~~~~~~~~~~~

That turned out to be the only positive result from their work. No foods remained on the counters when they'd finished two hours later.

"We've created a mess on the floor," Stephanie said. "I'd better mop up. Dad's cleaning service doesn't come again until next week." Carolyn and Martha watched from the doorway as Stephanie worked. She began in the corner in front of the refrigerator then leaned over to inspect a crack in the tile.

"This is new. I wonder what happened." She turned at the sound of Mr. Worthan clearing throat.
~~~~~~~~~~~

"Oh, hello, Dad. We hope you had a nice nap. Do you know what happened here?" She pointed to the broken floor tile.

"No, I don't. Maybe Marge did it. She could have dropped a pickle jar or something the last time she cleaned. I'll ask."

"It's right in front of the refrigerator legs. Does she move the appliance out to clean?"

"I don't think so. She's not very big. I doubt she could move it the way it's crammed into that space. It would take an elephant to get it out."

As she watched Stephanie, Martha had an idea. "The lab report notes they checked the tap water. Did they check the water line that comes through the refrigerator?"

"Dad, do you drink this cold water?"

"All the time. Or I did until you brought over the fancy bottled stuff."

"Let's take a sample from that spigot to the lab. It could be contaminated." Stephanie poured a small amount into a glass and sniffed. "I can't smell anything unusual, but we'll get it tested. Let's get your brother down here. He'll know how to look for fingerprints or whatever else we need to know."

~~~~~~~~~~~

"Good idea, Martha," David said. "Let's take a look behind the refrigerator." He put on gloves before moving heavy appliance away from the wall. "I'm sure the lab techs checked for fingerprints all around. It looks as if they dusted everything in the kitchen."

"Should we be cleaning up?" Martha asked. "We've hit about every surface in this room."

"It's been released." He began to shove the refrigerator from side to side, inching it slowly forward. They noticed one leg slid right into the new crack on the floor, making it larger. At last he managed to squeeze behind it. "Where do you shut off the
~~~~~~~~~~~

water, Mr. Worthan? I don't want water flooding the floor when I remove the filter."

"Under the sink. I'll do it." He turned, then stopped. "Now I remember. Some damn plumber was in here installing a water filter. He put it in that line that runs through the refrigerator."

"When was that?" David asked.

"Must have been the day I got sick," Mr. Worthan said. "I forgot in all the excitement."

"We need to get that water tested," Stephanie said. "Don't use it in the meantime."

"That would explain the broken tile, wouldn't it," Carolyn said. "And why the lab reports come back negative," she added.

"This has to be the unit I saw our phantom Mr. Logan, a.k.a. Sly, enter," Martha said.

"We need to question all the tenants," Carolyn said. "Do any others have newly installed water purifiers?"

"God! Am I giving my babies poison to drink?" Martha said.

"We'd all be dead by now, Martha, but let's look behind our refrigerator. We should be able to tell if a filter had been installed, then removed."

"And we can look in the units owned by the other women who died."

"We should get over to the courthouse to see the property files. Deeds and liens have to be registered to be effective."

"Which reminds me of the argument Sly and Byron had on the deck at the Slam Dunk Café," Martha said.

"I suppose these poor tenants borrowed money and gave whatever security they could to pay the special assessments," Carolyn said.

"All caused by a barely noticeable amount of salt in the air," Martha said.

"Have you noticed that big problems usually start with very small deviations?" Stephanie said. "The paintings I have to discard usually start with one small flaw in the design."

"That's why we engineers have to be so careful of details," Mr. Worthan said. "It's a big responsibility to sign off on plans and specs."

"From minute particles of salt solution you go directly to murder?" David asked.

"I do some of my best work when I'm ravaged by emotion," Carolyn said. "Anger or fear. Either one will do."

"Maybe that's why we appreciate Georgia O'Keefe's work," Stephanie said. "She immersed herself in the passion of love and was afraid of nothing."

"Yes, but art doesn't often lead to murder. Greed seems to be at the bottom of these crimes," Martha said.

"Or fear," Stephanie said. "Old people rightfully fear being left penniless. After all, they cannot go back and start their careers again, no matter how successful they have been in the past."

"Fear is the opposite of faith," David said.

"When did you get so profound?" Martha asked.

"Maybe I'm having an early midlife crisis."

"Which reminds me," Stephanie said, "Carolyn and I want to take you two to our favorite bar. You need to see where the natives hang out. We can shoot pool, eat hamburgers, listen to music, even dance. Did they teach you to dance at the academy?"

"Sounds wonderful," Martha said. "I'll run right over and ask Mrs. Wingate to babysit. When do you want to go?"

"Tomorrow afternoon. Say around four?"

"What's the dress code?"

"Whatever you happen to have on."

Friday, July 11th

Martha felt a rush of excitement when the doors of the bar swung inward. Most of the patrons were busy yelling at each other in order to be heard above the din of the TV sports shows. Tennis, baseball, skate boarding, football, and soccer each dominated a large overhead screen. One lone news channel ran a segment of soldiers patrolling in camouflage uniforms, which stopped Martha in her tracks. She scanned the screen for her Lucas. How she missed him! Even so she felt a blast of rejuvenation. The very air was full of zing and testosterone, ratcheted up by unbridled Friday night joy.

The oval bar took up the entire center of a pub the size of a basketball court. A polished pine plank floor laid on the diagonal provided the only apparent unity to the scene. Two gangly male bartenders in white shirts poured and mixed in a frenzy behind the counter, while three well-stacked waitresses in black minis raced back and forth to the surrounding tables.

At four o'clock in the afternoon a variety of characters leaned their elbows on the bar, filling nearly every stool. They clutched their drinks as if by tossing back alcohol they could regain whatever vital parts of themselves they'd had to forfeit during their week's work.

Carolyn had rightly defined the dress code. Some women wore swim suits with t-shirts pulled over them, more had come in skimpy denim shorts and very tight knit tops exposing both belly buttons and a deep cleavage. A few relaxed in classy suits or dresses they must have worn in the office that day. The clothes all looked glitzy to David's Midwestern eyes, unaccustomed as he was to sequins and beads on daytime wear. Men mostly wore blue jeans, but off in a far corner, men and women in dark blue, sweat-stained police uniforms sat around several tables they'd shoved together.

Carolyn led the way to a table on the right and spoke to people at nearby tables. It felt like a reunion. A waitress appeared instantly, bringing a pitcher of draft beer and a fistful of iced mugs.

"This could be anywhere in America," David said. "Same TV,

same din, same smells." For sure it wasn't Manhattan with its endless supply of Wall Street suits, but except for the swim wear and mini-tops, the patrons could be sitting in an Iowa tavern.

"It's our bars that hold us together," Carolyn said. "Forget the shopping malls and churches. This is the real community."

"Now you're being sarcastic," David said.

"Only to counteract your earlier philosophizing. Nothing serious happens here."

"A bit of serious mischief now and then," Stephanie said.

"A bar is a bar is a bar," Martha said.

Someone stood up in a far corner and stumbled toward them. Thomas Logan a.k.a. Sly Poltron. He dragged a chair from another table and sat down at theirs.

"Everybody here buys me a drink," he said. "You cost me a week's take." The wide smile on his face contradicted his edgy words. "Maybe more." He stank, he burped, his eyes gleamed red, and his cheeks sagged. "Goddamn police crawling everywhere over my business. Call 'em off. You got your damned TV back, now get off what's mine."

David picked up his chair and shoved it into the narrow slice of space between Carolyn and Sly. He gave Martha a penetrating look as he did so. If she read his message correctly, he intended to make good use of the chemicals Sly had slurped.

Alcohol often did as well as truth serum.

"Quite a business you have there, Sly," David said. "Best-looking pawn shop I've seen anywhere,"

"I agree," chimed in Martha. "Everything neat and dust-free. I'll bet your books are beautiful."

"No books. All on Quattro Pro and up here." He tapped the side of his skull with a forefinger. "Nothing gets past this polecat." Martha wished she could turn Lucas loose on that program. He'd find the funny business.

"No books at all?" she asked. "How do you file your income

tax reports? Isn't your store incorporated?" Sly ignored her question. She'd heard Lucas complain often enough that the IRS wouldn't take corporate tax forms electronically. She also knew what Sly was thinking: What does a woman know about taxes and business? He had other thoughts uppermost in his mind.

"Did you know me and your lady friend were quite a pair at good old Sunny High?" Sly's words rearranged his immediate future. Blood rushed to David's face as he fought for self control.

"It's hard to be in business these days," David said, after he'd stifled a purely Neanderthal response. "What with all the affirmative action, tax regs, and government snoops." Sly jerked himself up straight and slapped his hand down on the table top.

"Damn right! Government boys poking into every corner. Ought to string up all those crooks in Tallahassee. Nothing but trouble comes out of that stinking hole. Ought to blow up D.C., too. If I'd been flying that plane, I'd a hit Congress first. To hell with the Pentagon." A wall of silence dropped upon their table and extended into the space around them. Carolyn dug around in her purse, and pulled out a drawing pad and a pencil.

"Sit right there," she said, licking the pencil tip. "I'll make you famous. What a study in . . . " David had to guess the rest of the sentence spoken under her breath. That was when he realized his clean shave, short hair, ironed shirt, and pants that fit, were out of place in this bar. He might as well have had the FBI badge tattooed on his forehead. He looked around and saw mostly construction workers off in the middle of the afternoon because they'd started work before daylight. Maybe he should go sit with the police types. But no, he hadn't sweat enough today. Sly fit in, but he didn't.

"Sit still," Carolyn ordered. "Both of you."

"She does 'bossy' well, wouldn't you say? One of these days you'll see her cartoons in the New York Times," Stephanie said. "All the male characters look browbeaten, which they are. You're the first arrogant man she's ever been able to capture on paper."

"I'm usually too busy correcting my mistakes to be arrogant," David said. Stephanie followed his inquisitive glance at the other patrons.

"The guys in button-down shirts work at the Cape. They're engineers. When they leave, you'll see them drive off in light-weight pickups. The construction guys in denims own shiny hogs with big chrome pipes."

"The Cape?" he said.

"The space center on Cape Canaveral," she explained. "You know, the technology edge of the universe." Carolyn continued to draw. He felt his skin prickle as she eyed his torso. He imagined that she had mentally ripped off his shirt and sent the buttons flying. He'd pose nude any day for this artist. God, would he!

"Mr. Poltron," Martha asked. "tell me about your business. How do you make a profit on other people's goods while you're only holding them for a short time?" She wasn't distracted by what was going on around her. Maybe a clear head came with a happy marriage.

"Easy. Mostly people can't take their junk back. They bring it to me and spend the cash."

"Junk like engagement rings, unused guitars, keyboards, audio systems, champagne glasses?" David felt proud of his sister; she'd flattered Sly into rapt attention.

"Paintings and sculpture are big. Your lady here, she just wants the frames. The art is mostly junk."

"What isn't junk?"

"Jewelry, guns, sterling silver, crystal, antique furniture. In my business you have to know everything. Skateboards and wake boards are big now, nearly as hot as surfboards. After awhile I sell it. Everybody makes out. The landlord, which is me, the seller, which is me . . . "

"And the thief, which is you." David wondered what had possessed him to interrupt Martha's nice conversation. Was he playing bad cop to her good one? He had little time to muse before Sly grabbed for his neck with a pair of hands the size of dinner plates. Sly was fast but not fast enough. David stood, grinned at him, and raised two flattened hands.

"Don't mess with the feds, is that it, boy?"Sly sneered at him and tried to stand. The woman who appeared instantly beside him was petite, lusciously built, and pleasant. "Not here, boys. Go fight in the alley, but not here." The off-duty cops sitting in the back had already formed a phalanx and advanced solidly toward their table.

"Haven't you had enough trouble for one day, Sly?" the first officer said. "You know the rules: no trouble in Margo's place. I could go back and make a bigger mess in your store if you'd like." Martha, Carolyn, and Stephanie took their lead from Margo. They decided it was smile time, maybe even escape time.

"I apologize, ma'am." David sat back down and looked into his empty glass. Was he still smarting at the idea of Sly and Carolyn making out in high school?

"We're cool," Sly said, holding up his hands. Carolyn put away her drawing pad.

"Is that a wanted poster you're penning?" Margo asked. "Let me see it."

"Just a whimsy, Margo," Carolyn said, but she showed it to her. The woman must be nearly ninety, judging from the tiny lines around her eyes and mouth, but she still flaunted a Barbie Doll figure. It was easy to see how she kept the men in line, and the women customers would be too jealous of her tiny waist and incredible breasts to make trouble.

"I'll buy it," Margo said. "If either of these two shows up in here again, the bartender won't serve them. Final. Done. Out. You've spent your last dime in my place. Sly, we never want to see you again."

"There's other bars in this town if you're so high and mighty." He stumbled to the door, tripping on his own feet in an effort to achieve dignity.

"I should have kicked him out years ago," Margo said. "He's always picking fights, but you'll have to leave as well. How much for the drawing, Carolyn?"

"It's a gift to my favorite barkeep." Carolyn tore off the paper and handed it to Margo, who said thanks and tottered away on her four inch heels.

"Friends, I hope you agree it's time to go sit by the river and enjoy the evening," Carolyn said. "I know a place with plenty of dockside tables."

"This is a first for me," David said. "Kicked out of a bar."

"I wish I'd brought a camera. You should have seen Sly's exit. It had all the drama of an Act IV, scene four in a high school production."

"Is there someplace we can go in this town and not meet friends, relatives, or other assorted killers?" Martha asked.

"Follow me," Carolyn said, "into the darkening night."

CHAPTER 8

The Sundowner Café nestled close to the calm lagoon the locals called a river. Carolyn and friends took a table on the deck, ordered dinners, and admired the western sky. A gigantic orange globe hung above the horizon and reflected across the water.

"If we're lucky we'll see a pair of dolphins cavort along in the channel," Stephanie said. "When I was a kid, we could water ski down this stretch of river. Now it's all a no-wake zone. Good for the dolphins and manatees, bad for water sports."

"I've been told dolphins love to chase boats," Martha said.

"Yes. They romp in the bow wakes. But the manatees can't get out of the way fast enough, so they bear multitudinous white scars on their backs and tails."

"Lucas and I saw dolphins once when we took a tour boat out to Santa Catalina Island off the California coast. I swear hundreds of dolphins played around the cutter."

"Were you and Sly really a thing in high school?" David blurted out the question; he's stewed on it long enough. Carolyn laughed and patted his hand.

"In his dreams. He used to follow me around. He is so

pathetic." David wanted to ask about Timmy. Whose son was he? It made his skin crawl to think of Carolyn and Sly in bed together.

"This town is tighter than Elmwood Crossings," Martha said. "Everybody knows everybody else, and most are related."

"That's why my mother keeps getting elected mayor. She's the matriarch of the clan," Carolyn said.

"Speaking of your mother, does she have a new boyfriend?" Stephanie asked. They followed Stephanie's gaze toward a table even closer to the water's edge than theirs. The man had draped his dark jacket over the back of the chair. He leaned forward, earnest and determined about whatever he was telling his companion. The woman noticed their attention and waved. Mother Monica stood and walked to their table.

"Carolyn, have you finally met the man who'll make an honest woman of you? Introduce me. I'm the mother-in-law from hell and he should know it. Would he be a good father for my grandson?" Carolyn laughed.

"Get your friend over here, Mother, and join us. You can inspect David for yourself. Have you had dinner?"

"Hell no! We're not even finished with our drinks. Who needs food? The chef's not so great here; we eat his stuff just for the spectacular view. And if I sit near the water, all the customers see me, gossip about my dates, and I get their votes when I run again."

Carolyn's mother had flaming red hair that had been cut into a short cap; her figure had definitely not been allowed to enter the matron stage. She still looked as good in her miniskirt and string-strap top as any woman in the place. He could see where Carolyn got her looks, but what about the blond hair?

"Mother, who is the new man you're sitting so close to?" Carolyn asked. "I've not seen him around."

"Dr. Harvey Nelson. He runs the state forensics lab, and he's thinking of moving to our fair city when he retires next year. He brought over the lab reports on our elderly corpses. Don't you think we're better than any other shore city?" The last question was directed at David, but Martha answered.

"It's my first time in Florida, and I can't imagine anything nicer. Tropical beauty, sunshine, and exciting criminal activity." Mother Mayor laughed. "We have little enough of the latter. You just caught a winning streak. You must be the sister. What would you think of Carolyn as a sister-in-law?" Carolyn smiled. She must have had an interesting time of it as a teenager. None of her mother's verbal assaults pierced her enameled exterior.

"She's just the woman I've been trying to find for my brother. Self-assured, beautiful, smart, and talented. All the good qualities we need in our plain Midwestern gene pool."

"We've not even kissed," David said, "and you're talking about progeny. Did I miss something?"

"What's the matter with him?" Monica's face tightened into real concern.

"He's been badly burned," Martha said. "Needed skin grafts. Both the donor sites and burned areas hurt like hell. It'll take time, but Carolyn is perfect. I knew this trip to Florida would turn out well."

"You're my kind of woman," Carolyn's mother said. "Direct and to the point. I know where you stand. Would you move down here and become my city manager? I've just had to fire the third one in three years. You'd have a job until I get thrown out of office; unfortunately that could come any time now. In the meantime, it would give your brother plenty of reason to visit my daughter."

"Could we talk about something besides my relationship with Carolyn? Say, whether Iraq had weapons of mass destruction or the rights of Eskimos to shoot whales with Uzis." David punctuated his sentences with a lopsided smile, and Carolyn continued to look amused. Didn't anything ruffle her feathers?

"Let me get Dr. Nelson," Monica said. "He has a topic of interest." Before she could move, the waitress brought their food. Mother Mayor walked around the table inspecting each plate. "I'll take an order of what Stephanie has. It looks like a nice piece of snapper, and I like the hint of lime in the Monterey sauce."

Monica became considerably less combative in the company of the distinguished Dr. Nelson.

"I'm not sure I care to discuss your cases in the ambient glow of the evening," he said. "It's too beautiful here." The man's brown hair had a bristle of gray tips above his ears.

"It will darken in a few moments," Stephanie said.

"And I'll darken your spirits. No. Wait until tomorrow morning and read the reports. Nights with moonlight gleaming across the water are for love and romance."

"About those Eskimo whalers," David said. "Should they be allowed to use walrus-tusk harpoons or provided with nuclear weapons?" Everybody laughed, and no one volunteered to clue in the puzzled pathologist.

"What concerns me," said Carolyn, "is whether their homeowners insurance will cover injuries or other losses sustained while they're on the hunt."

"Good question," David said, "but I didn't realize one could get a policy on an igloo. See what a skilled conversationalist I am?"

"I'm sure it's the FBI training."

"Actually no. It's Speech 201, better known as debate. Pick a topic, any topic, and then argue both sides."

Saturday morning, July 12th

David's fantasy life galloped off across the mesa and brought him up sharply at the edge of a cliff. He deliberately sought out Carolyn and did it entirely without finesse. He pounded on the door of her father's unit at nine o'clock after he'd had his run, his coffee, his oatmeal, and made a phone call to his office. She opened the door wearing a long T-shirt. Maybe with a swim suit underneath. Doesn't anybody wear clothes down here?

He balled up his fists to keep from grabbing her.

"I have your mother's approval," he said, "so could I please take you out on a date?"

"And I have your sister's blessing. Come in." He stepped into the little entry hall but kept his eyes on Carolyn's.

"Does either matter?" Just keep breathing, he ordered himself. Slow and easy.

"No. Approval is supposed to come later, after much struggle." She kept up the sweet face, the knowing witch's smile. Stick to the plan. Don't throw her onto the floor and grapple. Don't even plant a kiss on those soft, inviting lips.

"Do you know a place with white tablecloths where waiters wear satin cummerbunds and bow ties?" he asked.

"Why?"

"I brought down a navy jacket and a starched shirt. So far, I've not seen any place here upscale from a hotdog stand. What I really need to look well dressed on the beach is a panorama of tattoos down my arms and across my back. Maybe under my trunks as well." David felt a growing discomfort at standing so close to her. The entry hall was too small for flight.

"About ten miles south," she said. "The Scarab. I have a strapless black dress. There's absolutely no place to pin a corsage, so don't bring one."

"It sounds as if there will be plenty of places to plant kisses." She flushed pink. "Is tonight okay? I know it's short notice, but . . . "

"You'll have to use my mother's name to get reservations on a Saturday night."

"That's preposterous. We can't just show up at the door?"

"That's how it is, and they'll check your references."

"I hope they don't call that Barbie Doll manager we met yesterday. I'm blackballed for life in her bar."

"She was putting on a show. What you should be worrying about is that I haven't had a date in years. Mother is desperate to get me settled with someone. Anyone."

"My sister wants instant cousins for her children."

"We'll have to make this one hell of an evening to accomplish their desires." His arms acted on their own and found her within their circle, pressed against him.

"Does the *maître d'* perform marriages, or do we need a ship's captain?" he whispered, but she pulled back and laughed.

"You're so naive! Even Florida has laws about matrimony so nobody gets tricked into it. Lust is not a good reason, and I am not a stranger to the baser emotions. I've been watching your eyeballs spin for days."

"You have a certain effect on me, which I've been trying to hide."

"Badly hidden. Sexual deprivation is written all over you."

"I would like it better if you saw me as strong, poised, and self-confident."

"What fun would that be?" Her wicked grin widened and her eyes sparkled with humor.

"So, what time do I pick you up?"

"Make the reservation for eight, pick me up at seven-thirty. Now go away. I'll have to arrange for nails and a pedicure. Maybe a massage. Certainly a long, comfortable soak in a hot tub."

"You're messing with my mind."

"Absolutely. You'll spend the day wondering which part of my body is being caressed." He found himself out in the hall as she closed the door behind him. He headed back to 506.

~~~~~~~~~~~
~~~~~~~~~~~

"Is it safe to leave you for three hours tonight, Martha?" David asked. "I've arranged to take Carolyn out for a late dinner. You're not to go messing with this criminal investigation while I'm away."

"I'll spend the evening with a book and the babies on one condition. You must get that forensics report from Dr. Nelson and let me read it."

"I'll see what I can do."

"Why not be direct? Call your friend Linda, the chief of police."

"Can you think of a good reason to do that? It's not as if she likes me."

"She likes me. We'll take her to lunch, and I'll agree to discuss her mother's job offer. We'd be working on the same team."

"You're not serious about moving to Sunny Shores!"

"No, but neither is Monica serious about hiring me. We'll have fun snowing each other and maybe I'll even get to see the report."

"I'm not comfortable with leaving Susan and Andrew with Wanda while we go to lunch."

"We can't have a serious discussion about murder with them around. Andrew picks up on everything we say."

"We can take them along and I'll drag them off to play on the beach while you two talk," David said.

"They'll be fine with Mrs. Wingate."

"Oh, I forgot. You're the perfect judge of character."

~~~~~~~~~~~

The aromas of soy sauce, spicy mustard, and hot peanut oil filled the air a half a block away from Ah Sin's. Inside, a half-dozen customers stood waiting to be seated, but after a nod from Linda, Martha and David were whisked across the crimson carpet to a corner table in the rear.
~~~~~~~~~~~

"I conduct most of my business in restaurants. It's not good for the figure but wonderful for relaxing tension. If you have to fire someone or make threats, best do it over number twenty-three, Chicken with Cashew." She unfolded her white cloth napkin and laid it across her lap as a dainty, smiling woman bowed and poured hot tea into small, earless cups. "When are you moving down, Martha?" Chief Elston asked. "The job is yours if you want it."

"You don't know a thing about me," Martha said, cuddling her tea cup up in both hands.

"Oh, I certainly do. University of Iowa for prelaw, Phi Beta Kappa; Drake Law School in the top ten percent of your class; seven years as an aggressive public defender; homebound with babies and bored out of your skull." Neither David nor Martha believed their ears.

"Computers are wonderful. We have so many legal problems out here on this sand spit. A lawyer would make a terrific city manager."

"What kind of legal problems?" That did interest Martha.

"The big developer v. small city kind. Those fellows are eating their way across our strip of sand like grasshoppers mowing down corn."

"I am flattered, but my husband joined my father's accounting firm when we married. We're settled for life in Iowa."

"Talk to both of them. We have plenty of business for accountants down here. Everybody is busy fighting off the tax man. We get your brother married to Carolyn and moved to Florida; then your father can have his entire family within an hour's drive. Dinner with the grandkids every Sunday. Nice."

"I begin to see why you're the chief," David said.

"That's right. Nobody can stand up to me. Never could. Ask Carolyn. I understand she's getting all prettied up for your date. I told her to wear red, but she's set her mind on black. Bad sign."

"Do I have any negotiating power at this table?" David asked.

"Might have. What do you want?"

"A look at the forensic report on the bodies we found on the beach and in the dumpster."

"You can damn well get them from your own outfit. Why bother me?"

"Humor me. You're easier." That riled the chief. She yelled her response loud enough so nearby heads swiveled their way.

"I am never easy. What are you giving up that I want?"

"I promise not to drag Carolyn back to Kansas City by her pony tail."

"You look the least like a cave man of anyone I've seen. Cave men I can find, but intelligent gentlemen don't grow on palm trees or wash to shore in empty whiskey bottles."

Martha nodded her head in agreement. "That's exactly the point, isn't it. The gene pool."

"Ladies, despite what you may think, I am not some sort of walking sperm bank. If all you want is good paternal genes for your nieces and nephews, you could shop online and purchase a young, blue-eyed Germanic type with a Ph.D. in physics. Please get yourself someone who doesn't burn in the sun."

"Now, now. Don't get nasty. Your sister and I will walk across the street while you pay the bill. She can scan the report on my desk while I turn my back and return phone calls." The two women walked out of Ah Sin's chatting like old college roommates while David waited for their check. What had he gotten himself into? Thoughts of Carolyn's generous smile and Buddha-like patience answered his own question. The woman was a growing mystery he intended to solve.

Saturday night, July 12th

David tried to concentrate on the traffic on A1A, but Carolyn's very quietness jangled his nerves. He had to say something. "How's Timmy? I haven't seen him since the first day we met."

"He's fine," she answered and fell silent again. Now that was strange. She didn't want to talk about her son. She wasn't making things easy. He glanced at her. Lots of bare shoulder, tanned legs, a slim body wrapped in a shimmery black dress, and as always, that enigmatic smile. He shifted his eyes to the car ahead that had slowed and set its blinker for a right turn.

"You want him kept out of our date," he said. She nodded.

"Your mother and sister have us producing an immediate sibling for him. Doesn't he deserve a say-so in the matter?"

"My mother has been making choices for me forever. Linda only recently got into the reclamation project."

"You don't mind?" David asked. She laughed.

The speed of traffic increased as they left the strip of beach condominiums and houses for the wide-open dunes and trisected flats of the air base.

"It's absolutely clear my mother and sister could make better choices than I have. They've set themselves the task of researching my prospects and found the local supply lacking in quality."

"Your choices were all bad?" Now that was interesting. He was an improvement over her previous boyfriends.

"There was the fellow grad student when I worked on my Masters degree, a fellow graphics artist when I worked in advertising, and currently an exciting, vibrant, and clever floral designer with fantastic entrepreneurial zeal." Cars driven by frustrated speeders kept passing David. His concentration split between getting to know Carolyn and mastering the road ahead. *Tread lightly*, he admonished himself.

"I don't seem to have gotten the knack of driving in Florida traffic," he said as a red sports car gunned past.

"Our highways are so crowded that we build up tension just walking to the carport. By the time we turn the key in the ignition, we're already furious." Her placid expression completely denied the road rage she described.

"So what happened to the grad student?"

"He switched to law, married a rich girl from south Florida, and now lives in a Ft. Lauderdale water-front penthouse."

"The artist?"

"Living in southern France. Wants to be the Van Gogh of the twenty-first century. Does drugs, drinks, and womanizes. Madly funny and purely mad. I think he's now in training to be a bullfighter part time while painting graceful students teasing frightened calves during his remaining hours."

"I'm too boring for you, Carolyn. No bulls, no drugs, moderate on the alcohol, and inept with women." For his humor and humility, he received another sweet smile. Wouldn't anything get her aroused? Be angry, be something! He was tired of carrying the entire conversational load.

"That's what my sister likes," Carolyn said. "After her initial dislike, she checked you out. Middle of your class in college, middle of your class at Quantico, middle of the road politics, and cross country team in your high-school year book. She's impressed. Old-fashioned, dogged determination, she calls it."

"Is your mother also searching for Mr. Humdrum?"

"That's doubtful. You've met her. We're getting close to Scarab's, so stay in the right lane."

"And the floral designer?"

"We're great friends. He works on cruise lines so is gone a lot, but we do things together when he's in port."

"He's my competition?"

"Not exactly. The truth is, I'm not the right sex for him. He thinks he's bisexual, but I doubt it." Their talk developed another sag. David tried to think of something comforting but couldn't. He launched a frontal attack.

"Your sister left something out."

"What was that?"

"Law Review. Top ten percent in law school."

"I hate lawyers, mostly." He sighed.

"That's not surprising, so let's talk about the art world."

"Let's talk about your marriage. I want to know the territory before I cross the border into it."

"I married my ex because it was the proper thing to do. We'd been dating for years. My family expected it. Her family expected it."

"And she said she was pregnant."

"Wrong. She was pregnant."

"What happened to the kid?"

"Stillborn."

"God!"

He had at last touched a nerve, but sympathy wasn't exactly what he wanted from her. He wanted to reach over and wipe away the tear making a slow path down her face.

"We floundered for years after that, determined not to fail."

"I am so sorry." The compassion in Carolyn's voice hurt. He felt his own tears begin to form. He raised his chin and cleared his throat.

"Turn here," she said, "into the driveway before the white sign."

~~~~~~~~~~~

David was unprepared for the attention given to them in the Scarab—a table up front near the piano with the musician fingering out a delicate piece by Brahms; two waiters filling their wine glasses; a vase of fresh white orchids between them; and a visit from the chef.

"Good evening, Carolyn. Good evening Mr. David. Let me recommend *tournedos buerre* and *pomme de terre à l'ail*," he said. The man was tall, thin, self-assured, and entirely enclosed in a white jacket and striped pants. His eyes danced with pleasure under the tallest white cap David had ever seen.
~~~~~~~~~~~

"Have we left Florida and flown across the Atlantic?" David asked. "I must not have been paying attention."

"*Oui, Monsieur*." The chef bowed and grinned.

"Whatever you suggest, Émile," Carolyn said.

"I'll have the same," David said. The apparition in white turned on his heel and sped away.

"You did want an appropriate place to wear your jacket, didn't you?" Carolyn asked.

"I feel like a fraud, as if I just wandered out of the corn patch. Where is my hoe to lean on? Where are my blue-striped overalls with one strap dangling? Should I light my corncob pipe?"

"When I see our imperious chef, I see the brat within, the most obnoxious boy at the pool, a splashing tease from morning to night."

"You're about to tell me you're a trained lifeguard. Is there anything you can't do?"

"Hang onto a man. That I cannot manage." David reached across the table and laid a hand over hers. When their eyes met, his filled with compassion.

"Been there," he said, "and it hurts." Carolyn left her hand curled inside his.

"The worst thing," she said, "is that I haven't really wanted to last with anybody." David nodded.

"I know. It didn't seem worth the bother to hang onto my ex. Emptiness is preferable to anguish. Sometimes you have to choose your pain." She sipped her wine and admired the clarity of the glassware in the gleam of light from the candle planted among their orchids.

"Yes. There are fewer peaks and valleys. Loneliness is a constant ache, not a stabbing pain; but I don't care for being alone at night in a cold bed." Her eyes met his, unafraid and honest.

"You have your son, your career, your passion for art, your work with students."

"True, and you have your passion for bringing criminals to justice."

"And protecting my fellow citizens. Don't forget that. Putting one thief in prison saves the household silver and jewelry of a couple hundred law-abiding citizens."

"How did you get interested in the FBI?" She sipped wine, not moving her hand from his. He was more interested in Carolyn than in the contents of his own glass.

"Some inspiration came from shows I watched on TV; then there was the body of the child found floating in the river near our town. Nobody ever caught the killer. He was the son of Estelle, the woman who cleaned for us. A fine mother who loved her son better than anything else in life. Even as a kid, I understood her love and felt her loss."

"That would do it," she said.

"We've gotten deep, haven't we. Ten minutes from casual to confiding."

"You're easy to talk to."

"And we have our losses in common." Carolyn turned her hand palm up and clasped long fingers around his wrist. He looked at the two hands entwined upon the table.

"You have strong hands—the tough, working hands of a sculptor. They communicate safety with their grasp." She looked up and released her hold.

"Here comes our food."

David was surprised at the size of the salad placed before him—small, centered on his plate, and beautiful. Watercress, a few slivers of radish, curled cucumber slices, red lettuce, arugula, and a drizzle of lemon dressing.

"I don't think this salad came from a cooler at McDonald's," he said.

"It's the freshness that counts. Émile practically goes out to the fields to pick them."

"Was he always Émile?"

"No, his true name is Simon, which gave us lots of reason to tease him when we played 'Simon Says.'"

"Everybody gets teased about something."

"Your name, too, Mr. David Santorino?" she asked.

"Oh, yes."

"And you've not gotten over it?"

"Absolutely not."

"I won't ask about your elves and reindeer," she promised "but what are their names?" David had long capitalized on his ability to deepen the dimple in his chin with a smile. He did it now and watched Carolyn openly admire his face.

"The real or imaginary ones?" he asked.

"Imaginary is fine. Let's stick to emotional truths and fictional people. That's the reverse of the rest of my life."

"But your art is real."

"Hidden, but always honest." she said. "You can't paint a lie."

"There's nothing honest about my life," he admitted. "It's all devious, manipulative, or downright sneaky."

"That's because you're trying to outwit real criminals, the most despicable of our fellow human beings."

"They might be *homo sapiens*, but I'd not call many of them human."

"Like whoever is killing the sweet little old ladies of Sunny Shores?" Carolyn asked.

"And worse. I've been dealing with a man who mutilated and ate children." David felt disgust rising from his gut. "This is not good dinner conversation." Carolyn leaned forward.

"Could I divert your mind from depraved murderers?" David stared at the swell of her breasts; his face flushed, and his breath caught in his throat.

"It might just turn me toward crimes of passion."

CHAPTER 9

An attentive waiter replaced their wine glasses and poured red wine. Elegant piano music covered the subdued clink of silver and china.

"What do you paint?" David asked, picking up his fork. "I've yet to see any of your work."

"Serenity. Calm seas, luscious gardens, happy children. I look within myself for peace, and paint it." His eyebrows lifted.

"That might be another name for denial. I thought you dealt in reality and truth."

"It's called making choices. I choose beauty and goodness over violence." He noticed the stubborn tilt of her chin and the sudden hostility in her gaze. Ah! He'd struck real emotion. David wanted to know what was beneath her compliant exterior. The musician looked his way and caught his attention. Was there a glass on the piano he was supposed to stuff with ten dollar bills?

"Did you go to school with the pianist, too? He looks lean and hungry."

"No, but he is good, isn't he."

"Anything special you'd like to hear?"

"I don't know enough about music to make an intelligent choice. It's all background and beautiful." He chided himself for probing, but he wanted her emotions exposed, raw and revealed. And that wasn't all he wanted to see bared, but he kept his words light.

"Well, then," he asked, "would you chose to split one of those chocolate desserts I see being wheeled our way?"

"Absolutely. You divide, I select."

"That worked at our house when Martha and I were growing up. Don't forget she and I are the children of a math teacher and an accountant. Everything was fair and even."

"Like life, right?"

"Like life should be but never is."

"It's possible to make a good reality out of life," Carolyn said. "Difficult, but possible." Words as enigmatic as her smile.

~~~~~~~~~~~

While he waited to sign his credit slip, he eyed the painting hung beside the piano. "One of yours?" he asked.

"Yes. Émile displays them for me. I make good sales from customers who are contented with his food and tipsy from his wines."

As they strolled to his car, David put his arm around her waist. He was back in high school on his first date. Sweaty, anxious, and overwhelmed by the desire to touch her.

The restaurant had been air conditioned to the point of being chilly, but in the hot, humid air of the parking lot he removed his jacket. He bent to kiss her before he unlocked the door, and groaned with shock as her fingers slid down his bare arm. Before he could hold her, she slipped away and climbed into the car.

Belted in on her side, she seemed remote, even cold. He started the engine.
~~~~~~~~~~~

"It seems we have opposite life views," she said. "I look everywhere for beauty while you seek the depths of evil."

"I hate these bucket seats. You're a mile away over there on the other side of the console."

"You're living in the past. Detroit has practically quit making front bench seats."

"A serious error."

"There's a wooden bench on the dune crossover near the air base. Wonderful in the moonlight for ocean viewing and sitting close."

"Tell me where to turn off." She did, but they found another couple snuggled on what should have been their bench.

"We could walk awhile," David said, "or maybe you don't want to ruin your dress."

"It's indestructible." They slipped off their shoes and held hands as they plodded across still-hot sand, but soon the damp, packed sand by the shoreline comforted the soles of their feet.

"This is not like my first date," David said, "and it's nothing like Iowa."

"Iowa seems far away."

"It is, both in time and distance."

"We've each had full lives since high school. Years of study and career building."

"It's as if I'm waiting for something to happen, marking time until my future arrives." Did each wonder if the other would be present in the days ahead?

"Look, somebody left us two beach chairs," she said. "They'll do for the present." Nearing low tide, the ocean lapped gently at the shore. They watched endless scallops of glowing froth pulse to shore, washing their feet with soothing water.

"The sea must be a large part of the peace and beauty that shimmer around you," he said.

"It is." After a bit she asked, "will Martha wait up for you?"

"I hope not."

"There's something I'd like to show you."

"Some etchings, perhaps?" He grinned into the darkness. "I can only hope."

"Two things actually, and both are in my dad's apartment." For answer he kissed the palm of her hand.

They ran across the sand to the car.

~~~~~~~~~~~

"The first exhibit is in the kitchen." Carolyn led the way, knelt in front of the refrigerator, and ran her hand over the tile floor in front of it. "Isn't this just like the broken tile in 501?" He squatted beside her, drawing close in the small aisle between counters. He could smell her hair, inhale her perfume. He ran his fingers over the break in the flooring, wishing it was her skin, her thigh, her . . . .

"Yes, it is," he said. "Did you get the water checked here?"

"I just found the break this evening before we left."

"And you've not tasted any water from this line?"

"No. I usually drink bottled water. I'll get this source examined in the morning."

"What else?" She looked puzzled until he added, "What else do you want to show me." Carolyn took his hand and pulled him through the living room and down a hall. She flipped on a light switch and David drew in his breath.

"Wow!"

"Is my dad proud of his daughter, or what?" Paintings hung on all four walls, floor to ceiling, the simple frames nearly touching each other. Red and yellows forms, black lines, orange and purple shapes—some clear in meaning, some to be guessed at. "What do you see?" she asked.

"A riot of color, the fireworks of joy that sings of excitement. It's a hymn to life, but it's not serene."

"These are from junior high school through my BFA and
~~~~~~~~~~~

MFA. The quietness came later." She turned and pointed toward the wall behind David, where the colors were more subdued. He saw an infant, a baby, a toddler, and a boy perhaps three, each surrounded with roses. "These are post-Timmy," she said. "Incidentally, he's spending the night with his cousins."

"You didn't want to talk about him earlier. Why now?"

"I wanted you to see how important he is to me. He's part of my deepest core. My art shows the devotion he's brought to me. Notice I surround him with a hedge of roses."

"Your roses have thorns larger than the flowers." She ran her hands around the picture of the infant, as if to gain reassurance from the sharp prickers.

"Yes, he's protected by beauty and by barbs."

David knew he had to ask.

"Which of the former . . . boyfriends is Timmy's father?" Tears welled up in her eyes. She reached for his hand and pressed his palm against her face.

"Timmy's mother left him in the trash behind the art building." He put his arms around her, letting her rest her face against his shoulder.

"You adopted him?" He whispered the question.

"Yes. He has a family—mine. I know who his birth mother is, Miss Allison Granby, and I worry constantly that she will make some sort of claim to take him away from me. The truth is, I paint the pictures to hide from my fear. If I expressed such dread in my painting, it would destroy me."

"So, it's possible to lie in a painting?" She nodded, her face still pressed against him.

"The paler works don't sell as well as the old ones," she said. "My timidity comes straight from my soul to the canvas. People buy courage and hope; rarely do they want to pay for anxiety."

"How realistic is your fear? Is it a legal adoption?"

"Yes. My attorney put notices in the newspaper for the required amount of time, asking for the father to appear. He also sent the required form letters to the girl. The father neither responded nor came to court. Allison is still around, gets visitation, watches me, watches Timmy, waits for me to make a mistake. I've thought of moving away."

"It's a crime everywhere to leave an infant in a dumpster."

"Yes, but I don't want her jailed." They'd been slowly circling the room, stopping now and then as David studied some aspect of a painting. He drew her closer, kissed her.

"The beauty of your paintings, the beauty of you. I'm awed, overwhelmed. Could we call this our second date?"

"Why?"

"I don't want to hurry you, but we seem to be heading for that massive futon in the corner."

"I know."

"It's not safe."

"What isn't? The futon?" He meant to say, "making love," but the words felt too dangerous, too honest.

"No, the water in the kitchen."

"I'm not thirsty. Are you?" He slid his kisses along her throat, sank on his knees to press his face against her.

"I'm awash, already filled, yet needy," he said. "Everything at once. Frightened, happy, elated."

"Should I turn out the lights?"

"No. This room is you. I want to be surrounded by you, within you, and totally with you." She knelt in front of him.

"It's me you want, isn't it? I've never been truly wanted for myself, but I feel that precious gift from you." Her eyes locked with his. "I know what it means to be the vessel of lust, but you want the vase as well. You want my emotions and my thoughts, not just the body they occupy." She ran her fingers across his lips. "You want more than flesh. You want my entire being, my soul. It's frightening yet magnificent."

"I've wanted you since that first glimpse on the beach. Hurray for beaches, those beautiful centers of romance! They could be covered with sand flowers for all I know, or maybe stars, or sparklers. Listen to me: I'm babbling for joy." She laid her hand across his mouth. He nibbled more kisses into her palm, shocked her with the intimate touch of his tongue.

"I need to feel your bare chest against mine." She began to unbutton his shirt. He sucked in his breath at the brush of her fingers, wanted to sag onto the bed and draw her with him as she undid the lowest button, groaned as she fingered his belt buckle. He reached down for the hem of her satiny black dress—it felt like a cloud in his hands.

"I want to be patient," he whispered. "I want to give you pleasure. You're making it impossible."

"Don't worry," she said, "save the patience for later. I want to meet your passion, all of it. Want me. Need me. Explode in me." For the first time, his hands caressed a woman who was not Mia, his lips kissed the nipples of a woman who was not Mia, and he'd at last found a woman who truly wanted him.

~~~~~~~~~~~

"What's a thousand miles or so," he said. Carolyn lay in the curve of his arm, clinging to his side, her breath blowing sweet and warm across the sensitive hairs of his chest.

"Over half-way to that other ocean," she answered. "Not far at all."

"We'll work it out," he said.

"There is something else you need to know. I have cats. Take me, take my cats."

"How many cats?"

"Three."

"That's lovely."

"No, they won't like you. You're sleeping in their half of my bed."

"Is that one of them over in the corner?" He pointed to a
~~~~~~~~~~~

canvas centered by brilliant green eyes within a ball of black fur.

"That's the first one when she was a kitten. Pretty, isn't she. One day she came wandering into the art department and stayed."

"So, you take pity on stray babies, stray kittens, and stray government agents. You have a magnificent heart."

"Now you can be patient," she said, "and be your FBI best. I want you to do the beautiful things to me I've read about, fantasized about, and never experienced."

"All of them tonight?"

"You have until dawn. Is that time enough?"

Sunday morning, July 13th

"What will you report to the mayor about our date?" David asked. They sat on the balcony overlooking the moonlit surf and sipped champagne. It was five-thirty in the morning. The night sky forecast dawn with a faintly lightened horizon.

"I'll say to her, 'We had a romantic dinner and walked barefoot on the beach in the moonlight. He is very nice.'"

"And?" He stroked the flesh of her inner thighs as he leaned over to kiss her breast. "What else?"

"I'll tell her you're unsuitable because you talk too much. I'll say, 'Go find me a man who believes in action.'"

~~~~~~~~~~~

The doorbell rang at seven.

"Who's there," Carolyn called.

"Police. Open up." A heavy fist pounded on the door.

"It's my sister," Carolyn said. "Do you think you could hide the clothes you wore last night?" She herself wore a black swim suit. They'd been for an early swim, and David had worn his
~~~~~~~~~~~

green plaid undershorts. They were in the kitchen having coffee, still dripping ocean brine. "I should have waited until later to call about getting the water tested. She's using this as an excuse to spy."

"She probably had a report about a nude bather. You shouldn't have yanked my shorts down."

"Sorry. I haven't gotten over my grade school urge to peek. I wanted to see if you shriveled in cold water."

"Want to peek now?" he asked. "You have my permission to grab my shorts any time." She ran her fingers across the flesh inside his waistband.

"Like this?" she asked.

"Carolyn! Open this door. I know you're in there. How does David look in the morning? The kids want to see his badge and his gun."

"She brought her children and Timmy." David raced toward the balcony. "No you don't!" Carolyn said. "Be brave."

When the door opened a crowd tumbled in.

"I didn't really have to knock," Linda said. "You know I have a key. Give me an A-plus for discretion."

"The coffee's ready. Did you bring the bagels?"

"That I did, and strawberry cream cheese. Pitch in, kids. When you've had enough, we'll head for the beach." Tangled sets of brown legs, skinny chests, and gleaming eyes jostled their way into the kitchen. Timmy grabbed his mother and she lifted him for a satisfying hug.

"Good morning. Did you have a nice time at Auntie Linda's house?" She nuzzled her head against his small chest. His legs began to swing. "Oh, are you too old now for mommy hugs and kisses?"

"Is he on TV?" Timmy pointed toward David, his brown eyes huge with wonder.

"Paulette told him David was like Howard on 'The Closers,'" Linda said. "He's taken the information to the next step, jumping to the logical conclusion. What a bright kid you have." Carolyn set him down on the floor.

"I know," she said.

"Nice swim trunks, David," Linda said. "That's just what I see the young twits wearing at the health club, although yours are a mite larger. From the looks of your unfocussed eyes, I'd say you two had a good night in bed. Congratulations!"

"Linda! The children!" Carolyn protested.

"Sorry. I forgot you're that primly puritan painter. God knows how you made it into my family."

"I'll just go get into some dry clothes," David said. "Excuse me."

"No need to lie or leave. Martha already told me you didn't come home last night. Nice work! All went according to my plan." Linda grinned and pulled a knife and cutting board from a drawer.

"Paulette, you're the oldest. Find the toaster and pop these bagels in after I slice them. Are we in a kitchen equipped with orange juice?" Carolyn lifted a half-gallon bottle from the refrigerator and put it along with paper cups, on the counter.

"Help yourself," Carolyn said, "but I don't need to remind you not to touch the water tap in the refrigerator door."

"We probably shouldn't be touching the refrigerator itself," David said.

"You're right, but there were no fingerprints on the handles or surface in 501. Fortunately, the perp didn't remember to wipe the inside of the filter. We found some good ones there and sent them off for matching."

In minutes the children had eaten every last bagel crumb.

"I'll take the kids to the beach while you do the clean-up," Linda said. She herded the high voices, wiggling bodies, and sacks of sand toys out of the condo. Carolyn and David faced each other in the disordered kitchen.

"Alone at last," he said. His words produced a slight frown.

"David, please don't take offence, but I have some things I want to do here in the condo. Would you mind helping Linda with the children?

"No problem," David said. "I'll go see if Martha needs anything, but first, we clean up." In minutes they'd thrown away the paper cups and plates, put the silverware in the dishwasher, and wiped the counters clean.

He went to 507, changed into swim trunks, and returned carrying Susan in the crook of his arm. Carolyn couldn't resist planting a kiss on the soft cheek of the gurgling baby. Would she someday have a sandy-haired cherub who looked like David's niece? The thought brought tears to her eyes.

"I'll be down later," she said. "I know Linda is responsible, and Paulette loves being Miss Little Mother, but I'm on edge when Timmy is near the water. He's absolutely fearless and loves to bounce in the waves. I'm always afraid he'll get knocked down and dragged out to sea. It would at the very least frighten him terribly."

"I won't let go of his hand. I promise."

"Thank you. I have the feeling faithfulness-to-duty is your middle name."

"David Faithful Santorino. For you, that is." He drew her close.

"Just looking at you sends my insides into a joyous tingle," she said. "All I can think of is going to bed."

"Did I fulfill a fantasy?"

"Several. Now get out of here so I can think." Carolyn slipped a loose T-shirt over her swim suit and seated herself before the laptop she'd placed on her father's desk.

When the Internet search engine came up she typed, "Colleges and universities," adding "Kansas City" to her request. Would there be an opening for an art instructor in the area? She dearly hoped so. Her family wouldn't like it, but moving away would solve two problems: being near David and escaping

Timmy's birth mother. She selected several colleges, then updated her work history. It had been five years since she'd looked for an academic position; she'd won a few prizes, had several shows, and taught a variety of art courses since then.

An hour later, with the arrow poised above the send button, she stopped to think. What would happen if she sent her resumé to the five schools she'd selected? All were within an hour's drive of Kansas City, and all had art departments. It was a big step to take. Did David really want her? Maybe he was just having a vacation fling. It was late to be applying. Universities usually staffed in the spring. Her fingers stopped. Should she talk to him first?

The doorbell rang. She sighed and hit the send button. She'd never been big on impulse control.

CHAPTER 10

"Hi, squirt." Sly Poltron stood outside Carolyn's door holding framed pictures under each arm. He'd really bulked up since high school. Was he wearing lifts? "These came in today," he said, "left over from an estate sale. I thought you could use them."

The last time she'd seen him, he was furious. Today he was Mr. Helpful.

"Good morning, Sly. It's nice of you to think of me. Let me get my purse so I can pay you."

"Hold on! Aren't you going to ask me in for a cup of coffee?"

"Help yourself to whatever's left in the pot. The mugs are in the cupboard above the coffee maker." She waved him toward the kitchen. "Put the frames down anywhere. I'll be right back." Now whatever had brought him here?

Carolyn exited the Internet and shut down her laptop before getting her purse. She found Sly stacking the frames in the front hall closet.

"You do make yourself at home," she said. "Are you checking out my dad's housekeeping?"

"Keep your shirt on. I've been putting frames in this closet for years. Where do you think he got the ones on his guest-room walls?"

"I had no idea, but grab your coffee and let's head for the beach," Carolyn said. "Linda's out there with the children; I promised I'd be right down to help keep track of them."

"It's tempting, but I'm a working man. Those stupid cops left a mess. It'll take a week to get things back in order."

"How much for the frames?" she asked

"Your dad paid me ten bucks apiece." Sly grinned.

"Fair enough. The materials cost more than that even if I make my own." She dug into her purse for her billfold.

"How's your work going? Are you still exhibiting?"

"I'm registered for a booth at the Sunny Shores Art Fair on Thanksgiving weekend. That's a good market for my kind of art."

"Good market for me, too. Customers wander in wanting to know what's inside a pawn shop. I nearly always manage to sell them some jewelry. My stuff is cheaper and better than the crappy trinkets they sell in the street stalls."

"Well, then, thanks for bringing the frames. If you won't come along, I'll head downstairs." She moved toward the door. Would he take the hint and leave? Instead, he plopped himself onto the nearest sofa and spread his arms out over the back.

"Not so fast. You need to listen." Sly's grin had not once left his face.

"Five minutes, Sly. For old time sake, I'll give you that." Carolyn looked at her watch.

"I can get your brother arrested for murder," Sly said. "Does that stop your clock?"

Byron was fragile, probably an alcoholic, but off of drugs for the first time in years. Carolyn knew it wouldn't take much to turn him back into the deadly swirl of using both. But she couldn't give Sly the upper hand.

"If he murdered someone, the police will find out, and nothing I can do will save him."

"Oh, but you can. I've always wanted you, and I'm between wives. Convenient. You need to protect your brother, and I'm without a bed partner." Carolyn hoped the disgust she felt didn't show on her face but sensed it did. The fatuous grin on his face curdled.

"I'm sure you're very good in bed, Sly," Carolyn said, "but that would be like incest. We grew up together. We're too close." Carolyn thought she'd given a great response—tactful, flattering, and dishonest in the extreme.

"Bullshit! We didn't even live on the same planet in high school. I was one of the groveling *outs* and you were a hottie." He stood. "You've had your chance." Suddenly, her knees felt as if they'd been filled with blobs of gelatin. "It's a good offer, Carolyn. Think about Byron's health before you turn me down. He couldn't stand doing time. Didn't I hear he tried suicide in high school?"

She still had bad dreams about the noose she'd found hanging from the garage rafters and the sight of a skinny Byron placing it around his neck. He'd kicked out the stool as she ran toward him, but her calls brought the neighbors; he'd been cut down and revived.

"I'm heading for the beach," she said. "If you can implicate Byron, you'll have to do so. I can't undo whatever he's done. Be sure to lock the door behind you." She dropped fifty dollars on the coffee table and walked to the door.

Sly went to the closet and pulled out David's jacket.

"I see your new boyfriend has taken up residence," he said. "Here I thought you were Miss Ice-in-the-Veins."

"That must be my dad's." Sly held it in front of his chest and measured a sleeve against one arm.

"I don't think so. What's the matter, none of us hometown boys good enough for you?" The sneer on his face and the scorn in his voice sent shock waves through her brain. This man harbored a ton of anger. Was he as dangerous as Martha thought? Maybe he had poisoned Stephanie's dad. Had he also laced her own drinking water with ricin?

~~~~~~~~~~~

She raged with growing fury as she trudged across the sand toward Linda. David had the children with him in the surf. Paulette held Timmy by one hand, and David gripped the other. Lovely! Andrew was attached to David's left arm, bouncing with glee. The Sunday crowd had picked up; she found herself surrounded by a mass of tan skin, colorful towels, plastic coolers, and hot radio music.

Martha and Linda sat under an umbrella with Susan. Carolyn dropped to her knees beside her sister.

"Do you think Byron killed Agnes and those other two women? What can we do?"

"Calm down, Carolyn. What happened?" Linda sat up and looked at her sister.

"Sly just demanded I move into his bed. In return, he won't implicate our brother in the murders."

"I'll kill him myself. Where is he?" Linda's muscles tightened. She stood in one abrupt motion.

"I left him in Dad's unit. I was so mad I didn't even wait for him to leave."

"You watch my kids. I'll see to that slime ball." Linda stormed across the sand and into the building.

"I couldn't help overhearing," Martha said. "That man should be rowed out to sea and dropped overboard with a big chunk of concrete attached."

"Don't think I haven't thought of doing that many times over. He continually harassed the frightened kids on the fringe. Loved nothing better than to make a shy kid cry. My brother was a softie who never could get the macho thing right even for show."
~~~~~~~~~~~

Susan began to whimper. Carolyn picked her up. It would be comforting to hold a baby . . . but this baby smelled.

"Time for a change, Martha. Sorry to be the bearer of bad news."

"It's also time for her morning nap. I'll take her in. Will you tell David where I've gone? He watches over me like a matron in a prison."

"Sure," Carolyn said. "I'll lie here in the sun and try to simmer down. Honestly, I've never been so angry in my life. That man is going off the edge and wants to drag a few others with him."

~~~~~~~~~~~

The elevator doors opened to an empty hall, but the jacket hanging on 507's door knob spoke volumes. Martha knew better than to touch it; ugly slashes ripped it from shoulder to hem and left it unfit for anything but Halloween wear. Her brother could go costumed as an out-of-luck bum or a corn-patch scarecrow. Carolyn wasn't the only enraged person around. Martha reversed her path and headed back to the beach.

Linda had returned and stood beside Carolyn, hands on hips, chin thrust forward, yelling so Martha could hear from twenty feet even over the roar of the surf and throb of boom boxes.

"It's him or me. He can't mess up my town, turning it into a theft ring and God knows what else."

"All you have on him is suspicion." Carolyn sat on her towel biting her lips and clutching one knee to her chest.

"You're right, but I'll get him. We'll do his store again. He never was at the head of the class, and I know he made a mistake somewhere."

"Linda, what did the lab report show about my kitchen?"

"Nothing! The water's pure as hell coming out of the refrigerator. "
~~~~~~~~~~~

"That's good!"

"No, it is not. We've got to get him red handed."

"I hate to butt in," Martha said, "but you have something else to examine." She told where she'd found the ripped jacket.

"It was in my dad's closet and in one piece not ten minutes ago. It has to be Sly's work," Carolyn said. "He was the only one there."

"Sly wasn't there when I arrived," Linda said.

"No matter, your lab techs need to look at the jacket," Martha insisted.

Perhaps David sensed the tension in Carolyn's body and Linda's combative stance, or perhaps the kids had worn him out. He walked toward them carrying a small boy under each arm; Paulette dragged her boogie board.

"You both look serious. What's up?" he asked. Martha described the ruined jacket.

"It triggers an old memory I'd nearly forgotten," Carolyn said. "In high school I was forever finding shredded coats in my locker. I thought someone was playing a mean joke."

"Were they your own clothes?"

"No. There'd be sleeves or pockets from miscellaneous jackets. Sometimes just buttons. The only problem was I always made sure to engage the lock. I never knew how anybody could get inside, but I didn't leave anything of value in it. Who'd want my books or class notes?"

"It's almost as if Sly wants you to know, isn't it."

"He thinks he's big and powerful."

"Something must have frightened him back in high school," Martha said.

"My dad would do it," Carolyn said.

"Dad owned the bank that held the mortgage on Sly's dad's business and on his house on Merritt Island," Linda added.

"He played a dangerous game if he was breaking into your locker," David said. "I'm surprised he didn't get caught."

"He hated it that my dad owned a bank and his had a debt-ridden pawn shop," Carolyn said. "It put Sly on the fringe of a suspicious element."

"The big shots in town were astronauts, NASA engineers, and scientists. Heads of programs and stuff like that," Linda said. "A banker was nothing. Besides, an East Coast chain bought Dad out around the time I graduated."

"I can connect the sliced jacket to Carolyn's turn-down, but not to the bodies we've found," David said. "That's a new realm of activity."

"Sly claimed he could pin murder on Byron," Carolyn said. "I assumed he was referring to the bodies we found. I'm worried. My brother is unsteady as it is." A high young voice interrupted.

"Are you talking about that creepy old guy who hangs around outside school?" All eyes turned to Paulette. A sturdy child still at the rounded, no-waist stage of life, she had been ignored while the adults discussed Sly's threat. She wrapped herself in a towel and squeezed water out of her ponytail.

"Paulette! You've never told me about it." Linda looked as fierce as the proverbial dragon, but the girl didn't flinch.

"You don't know everything, Mother. Ask any kid at Jefferson. We all talk about him. He's the guy who owns the pawn shop. He sells things to the little kids to get their lunch money. You know, cute erasers, giant pencils, toy cars, pencil sharpeners. That kind of stuff. He's creepy."

"I'll talk to you later, Miss Paulette. For now let's get the lab boys working on the jacket. There should be fibers in Dad's unit if he made the slashes there."

"Good job, Paulette. I've always known my favorite niece was a genius. Runs in the family, doesn't it?" Carolyn gave Paulette a nice hug and planted a kiss on the top of her head.

"You didn't buy anything from Sly, did you sweetie?" Linda asked. She'd altered her voice to soothing and motherly, a tone David didn't imagine she possessed. Paulette shook her head.

She wavered between tears and smiles. It wouldn't be long before the girl would be in the teen years when such labile emotions were a daily part of life.

"I still need to get a fresh diaper on Susan," Martha said, "but I can't get into our unit without disturbing the evidence of the town jacket." Linda pulled a cell phone from her beach bag.

"You can as soon as my lab techs finish. They'll be getting overtime pay this month," she said, "and I'll catch you-know-what from our treasurer when she has to write the checks."

"Where is that diaper bag I usually see you dragging around?" David asked.

"Inside the apartment. I was in such a hurry to get to the beach this morning that I came off without it." The group moved up the steps over the dune and rinsed off in the outside showers.

~~~~~~~~~~

"I hope you don't want another dinner at The Scarab," David said. "No jacket means no classy restaurant."

"Truly, I don't," Carolyn answered.

They sat on the floor playing Candyland with Andrew and Timmy. The boys rolled the dice so vigorously that she had to dive under the sofa for them after each throw. Their giggles had reached excited peaks topped only by the joyous gleam on their faces.

"I'm ready for lunch," David said. "What's in the kitchen?"

"There's plenty of bread and lunch meat here," Martha said, "and also the stuff I put in the cooler. Did you know it's barely eleven?" David opened the refrigerator.

"I see peanut butter and hot dogs. Do we need anything else?"

"Dig around. If you add baby carrots, apples, and raisins, you have a balanced diet."
~~~~~~~~~~

"I'm surprised you didn't offer me Kool-Aid," David said. "Mother poured so much down us it's a miracle we didn't turn the color of strawberries."

"My mother did that, too," Carolyn said. "I asked her why one time and she muttered something about cost per glass. Sugar must have been cheap in those distant days." They abruptly stopped talking when a determined shriek resounded from the bedroom.

"Susan says she has finished her nap," Martha said.

"I should have kept the boys quieter," Carolyn said. "I'm sorry."

"No apology needed. I'm glad to see my son so happy. Andrew usually plays alone, and he needs the companionship."

"I'll think of something less stimulating after lunch. Hungry, boys?" When two heads nodded, she added, "Go see Uncle David in the kitchen."

The sun had moved far enough westward so that the building itself shaded the eastern balconies. They sat around the little table to eat their sandwiches and watched the surfers glide to shore.

"Timmy and I need to head back to Oveida this evening. I teach a drawing class first thing tomorrow."

"Could Timmy stay here with Andrew?" Martha asked. "They really do seem to hit it off."

"He's enrolled in a summer program at the park district. I hate to have him miss that. They're doing tumbling activities, which he loves." Timmy jumped up and dashed into the living room. He began a series of somersaults across the floor, not stopping until he banged his heels into the television set. He grinned.

Carolyn corralled him for a hug.

"Good job, Timmy. Good job." She returned to Martha. "You've made a generous offer. What if I pack a little bag for him when I come back on Wednesday afternoon. He can stay here with Andrew until Saturday."

"That's the day we leave," Martha said. "You don't live too far from the airport, do you?"

"No."

"Then we'll drop Timmy off on the way over." The talk of departure cast a long shadow across David's face. Martha gazed from one stricken expression to the other, then took each child by the hand.

"Come on inside, boys. It's story time. Because you've been so good, you get to hear *The Cat in the Hat*." Martha closed the sliding glass doors, leaving Carolyn and David outside. David reached into his shirt pocket and pulled out a folded piece of paper.

"This came in awhile ago," he said. "What do you think?" Carolyn smoothed it out on the surface of the table and began to read.

"What is it? I thought it would be the lab report. It's just a bunch of Florida cities, some of them starred."

"It's a list of FBI offices in Florida. The marked ones might be able to use me. I've applied for a transfer."

"When did you do that?" she asked.

"When I went down for my swim trunks." Tears flooded Carolyn's eyes.

"I don't know whether to laugh or cry, but I have my own surprise. It's also a computer print out."

She pulled papers from her pocket and handed them to David. He read a few lines and ruffled through the sheets before he spoke. "My God! It's colleges in the KC area and a copy of your resume. Did you send this out?"

"To every one. Five. I don't know if there are any openings, but . . . " She leaned her head against his shoulder. "Do you mind?" He drew her closer.

"Do you remember that Poe story about the woman who sold her hair?"

"She sold it to buy her husband a chain for his watch, and he sold his watch to buy a comb for her hair. Did I get the plot right?"

"Close enough," he said. "It's a bittersweet love story I've never forgotten."

"And it's what we've done for each other. I feel a pull from a mysterious hand at work here."

"Putting us together out of all the other people on earth?"

"Something like that," Carolyn said. "Did you feel as bad as I did when Martha mentioned returning to Iowa on Saturday?"

"Devastated. I don't want you out of my arms."

"I'll probably end up in Kansas City with you transferred to Orlando," she said. David laughed.

"We won't let that happen."

CHAPTER 11

Wednesday afternoon, July 16th

When Martha opened the door, Timmy rushed through it and began to tumble across the carpet. Carolyn trailed him, holding his suitcase and a beach towel under one arm; she clutched a flat package in the other. "Whoa!" she called. "Don't you want to say, 'Hello'?" Timmy grinned at David and tumbled some more. Damp brown hair fell across his forehead when he stopped.

"Let me help you with those," David said and reached for the bag and package. She let him take the satchel but held on to the box.

"Not yet," she said. "It's a surprise." David's face colored beneath his freckles.

"Oops! Sorry, but I hope it's what I think it is."

"Did you bring two of them?" Martha asked.

"It's a chocolate cake," Carolyn said, turning the package upright.

"Yeah, right," Martha said.

"Cake," squealed Timmy. His eyes glistened.

"Sarcasm is wasted on the young," Carolyn said and turned to her son. "No, Timmy, we're just making grown-up jokes. It's not a cake. Remember not to tell. It's a secret."

"I was heading for the beach," Martha said, "and it looks like Timmy is ready. May I take him with me?" Timmy jumped up and down.

"By all means," Carolyn said. "Now slow down, son, and give Mommy a hug. You must mind Martha. Do everything she says. Okay?" The boy nodded, his eyes brilliant with joy. Andrew raced in from the hallway and did his own somersaults.

"I'm afraid you'll have your hands full with these two," Carolyn said. "They're a couple of firecrackers."

"I'll help, so don't worry about them," David said. Martha popped Susan into her stroller and knelt to fasten the straps.

"Come on, boys. Beach time. Bring your towels." Martha hung a net sack of toys on the handle of the stroller, and David opened the door. "I'm getting the hang of this, don't you think? I'll be all set if you'll bring the cooler down later. It's stocked with cold drinks and snacks for the kids. Once I get out in the great Florida sunshine, I won't want to come back inside."

"Cake!" Timmy shouted.

"Later!" Martha answered. The boys trailed her down the hall toward the elevator. Timmy skipped and Andrew hopped.

"Is Timmy precocious?" David asked. "He's very well coordinated."

"He's nearly four."

"Enough talk about the kids. I've missed you." He pulled Carolyn into the circle of his arms. "God! How I've missed you."

"It's only been two days," she whispered.

"I suppose you were too busy to think about your poor lovelorn David wasting away over here in Sunny Shores."

"It's nearly the end of the first summer session. I have a few reluctant artists to prod into finishing their projects; but no, I wasn't too busy to think about you." She stepped out of his arms and shoved the package toward him. "Take a look. It's something to remember me by when you're back in Kansas City."

"You wrapped it too well. Let me get a knife." David headed for the kitchen, where he slit the paper neatly along one edge. He drew out a framed portrait of three cats. His face sagged with disappointment.

"I hoped it would be a self portrait," he said. "When did you paint this?"

"I finished it yesterday, and the cats are even better. They sleep in my bed."

"Oh, I get it. I'm to morph into a kitten."

"Something like that. Do you like it?"

"I do, but I'm a bit surprised. It's bright and happy like the work you did before Timmy came into your life."

"When I started to paint Monday afternoon, I discovered I'm not the same artist you met a week ago. I'm confident now and able to handle life in all its many colors."

"That's what love does, isn't it. Explodes the boundaries."

"I'm bursting with vibrancy, and I don't think it's just because you're an FBI agent."

"What do you mean?" David asked.

"It's true your job makes me feel safer about keeping Timmy." Carolyn patted David's cheek. "I'd have the awesome power of the law on my side if Allison tried to take him away."

"Oh."

"Don't look so gloomy. It's more than your job. Art rises from places unrelated to intellect. The colors flew onto the canvas of their own volition, and they bubbled up from deep inside me. They're joyous and free. What you have done is remove the fear that's dogged my art for nearly four years."

"I think you've done the opposite to me—snatched away my freedom." David reached for her hand.

"That doesn't sound so nice either."

"I'm tethered by an unbreakable chain. It's invisible but

incredibly strong. Sort of like this." David pulled a small box from his pocket. "Would you care to open it?" Carolyn picked at the gold ribbon and fingered the gold-embossed paper. She raised her eyes to his.

"You're taking my breath away. I didn't expect a present on a Wednesday in July."

"It's as if we're reading each other's minds," David said. "Connection at a deep, deep level."

"Knowing the other's needs without being told." Her hands trembled.

"Open it," David pleaded. Carolyn did and stared down at an amber scarab. "It's to remind you always of our first date," he said. "Do you like it?"

"I love it. I'll wear it forever."

"Did you notice that it's the color of the gold flecks in your eyes?"

"I noticed that the chain is strong and goes with the others I wear."

"Your chains were one of the first things about you that caught my attention." Carolyn fingered her necklaces.

"Most of them belonged to my grandmother. She adored gold, and Grandpa loved giving it to her. Linda has as many as I do, but she chooses not to decorate herself while she's in uniform. I think she's afraid of being garroted with her own jewelry."

A sharp knock sounded along with a cry, "Open up. It's the police."

"Speaking of the devil, your sister called earlier and said she was on her way over." David opened the door.

~~~~~~~~~~

Chief Linda Elston marched into the kitchen and poured herself a cup of coffee before she sank onto a chair. David and Carolyn followed and stood together in the doorway.
~~~~~~~~~~

"Hi, Carolyn," Linda said. "Where's Timmy?"

"On the beach with the others; we're headed there shortly. But you look discouraged."

"Well, here's what's happening. Sly's fingerprints showed up inside the water filter in 501," Linda said, "and I obtained a warrant for his arrest,"

"So, he's in jail." Linda shook her head.

"When we got to his house, the place had been emptied. The store is closed, his bank account is empty, and he's vanished."

"How could he leave so quickly?"

"Let me guess," David said. "The truck he claimed belonged to him did. How else could he get everything moved out of his house?"

"The neighbors didn't see anything?" Carolyn asked.

"He lives in the middle of an orange grove at the end of a lane," Linda said. She took a swallow of her coffee. "There's nobody around to see his loading up or leaving."

"What about the store?" David asked.

"The valuable small stuff—diamonds and other jewelry—is gone. We've since learned the store and its contents are mortgaged to the hilt."

"So he left nothing of value." Carolyn sat on an empty chair. "Nothing except the bodies." Linda laughed unpleasantly at that comment. "Those old ladies had willed their condo units to Sly. When the matters clear probate, he'll own three units in our building."

"Doesn't Byron have a prior deed for those same units?"

"That's why the estates are being contested. Our brother didn't bother to record his deeds."

"So, why did Sly leave?"

"I have to assume someone on my staff told him about finding his fingerprints in the filter." Linda was a faded remnant of her usual powerful self. She sagged against the back of the chair. "I've been done in by my own people." Her news hadn't had time to settle before the door opened and Martha came in with Susan. She looked around.

"Where are the boys? Aren't they here? They got on the elevator ahead of me, but the door closed before I could get the stroller in."

"We haven't seen them, but why are you back so soon?" Carolyn asked.

"I forgot the sun screen. I suppose they're playing with the buttons, going from floor to floor, and giggling like mad," Martha said. "I'll go find them."

"That doesn't sound right," David said. "If they were still in the elevator, how did you get up here?" He followed her into the hall. The elevator lights indicated level one, and the hall was quiet. Martha pushed the button to bring up the cage. The doors opened to reveal an empty box.

"I'll go up the stairs and you go down," David said. "We'll catch those little rascals and meet back here."

"I've never spanked Andrew," Martha said, "but this just might be the day." Carolyn followed David and Martha through the stairway exit door.

"And here I thought I was doing something nice for Timmy, letting him spend two days with his new friend."

"Relax," Linda called from the doorway. She held Susan in her arms. "They're just being kids. Check to see if they're hiding under the stairs."

~~~~~~~~~~

When the three adults met again in front of the elevator, they had no boys in tow.

"I'll check the parking lot," David said.

"And I'll cover the beach," Martha added. "Where could they have gotten to?"

"Oh, Lord! Not the highway! Timmy loves to get ice cream at
~~~~~~~~~~

the 7-11 across the street. Surely they wouldn't . . . but I did give him five dollars to spend while he's visiting you." Carolyn's face had turned ashen, her eyes filled with horror.

The faint sound of a siren whined in the distance as all three piled into the elevator.

When they reached the street the fire truck had passed, and there was no sign of the little boys. David and Carolyn sprinted across the highway. Inside the convenience store, they tore up and down the aisles but found no Andrew and no Timmy.

Back outside, David reached for Carolyn's arm.

"We've got to stop running around and use our heads." he said.

"Mine is spinning. Sly's leering face jumps at me like a horror movie. Would he use Timmy to get at me?" She shook her head. "Surely even he wouldn't hurt the children."

"We don't know that Sly took them. I'll check with Martha on the beach," David said.

"What if someone finds them and tries to call," Carolyn asked.

"One of us needs to stay by the phones in your dad's unit and in ours."

Three police cruisers swung into the parking lot with sirens blaring just as David and Carolyn raced back across the street. David asked the officers to check inside with Carolyn. She carried the keys they'd need. When he moved to the ocean side of the building, the hot serenity of the beach stopped him in his tracks. He felt as if he'd just wakened from a nightmare. Several families played in the surf while others relaxed on the warm sand. Martha could be seen talking to one group, then dashing to the next. David worked his way toward her, stopping at each person he encountered to ask about the boys.

When he reached Martha she burst into tears and fell into his arms. "Nobody has seen two little boys by themselves. They saw them with me earlier, but not since we left the beach." She struggled to talk between sobs. He patted her back and endured again the terrible weight of his own uselessness.

"Carolyn and six policemen are searching inside the building," he said. "You need to get back to Susan so Linda can do her job."

"Are there any trash chutes in the building? Do you think they could have gotten themselves locked into a closet or something?"

"Neither one of them is strong enough to open the heavy emergency doors or tall enough to open any kind of trash drop. Besides, I've been carrying the trash outside. I haven't noticed any drops."

"A mail drop? Is there one of those? Kids can get stuck in the darndest places. They're so curious." David took his sister's arm and was warned by the electric tension of her tight muscles.

"Come on inside with me. Try to stay calm." His voice had softened to a comforting level.

"Go check the elevator," she begged. "Is there a way they could have fallen under it? How could I ever have let them get in without me?"

"Don't blame yourself. It doesn't help. You're the most dedicated mother I know, and you did not cause this problem. Besides, they'll turn up safe and sound." Stress had him speaking in clichés when he needed to be accurate and clear. Their building had already yielded three bodies and one poisoning—now two missing boys. He was an FBI agent. He kicked himself for sidestepping the very real crimes.

He'd wanted a relaxing vacation, wanted to avoid conflict and crime at all costs. Now he'd been thrown into the action whether he wished it or not. Could he have prevented the latest tragedy if he'd acted sooner? He'd never forgive himself if anything happened to Andrew and Timmy. Had Mia left him because he was so self-centered? Stuff it! This is no time to wallow in guilt.

~~~~~~~~~~~

Sly Poltron eyed the two boys sitting side-by-side on his brown leather sofa. They licked chocolate ice cream cones that would shortly begin dripping onto his expensive upholstery. He'd always said he wanted boys of his own, but when his first wife hadn't conceived and had insisted on virility tests, he'd learned about his low sperm count. "Drugs!" she'd yelled. "You give 'em up, or I'm out of here." But what the hell. He worked long days at the store, bought his wife all the clothes and booze she wanted; nights were for soothing relaxation, blanking out.

It was unbearably hot in the truck, but he'd just installed an air conditioner. Soon he'd quit sweating. The space he'd rented in a campground beside the Indian River had an electric hookup. The lack of windows proved to be an advantage.

This slow time of year brought few others to the campground, but even so, no snoopy neighbors could see inside. He'd plugged the floor lamp into a heavy orange extension cord. His microwave oven did all the cooking he needed, and the little refrigerator kept his beer cool.

Why the hell had he grabbed the two boys? He could already see they would make trouble for him.

The meeting with Byron hadn't gone well, and the kids had run into the elevator while he had his fingers poised on the up button. Why hadn't he just hit the door open button and left the place? Even in the dim light, he could see tears welling up in their eyes and trickling down their sweaty cheeks. He'd wait until dark, take that old rowboat he'd seen tied to the dock, and dump them in the river.

One thing he knew about himself—he was good at making the best of a bad situation. Isn't that what he'd been doing all his life? What did he want that these boys could give him? He'd better think of something before they drove him nuts with their whining.
~~~~~~~~~~~

~~~~~~~~~~~

The phone call came shortly after three. Carolyn jumped at the sound, but waited for a nod from David before she picked up the receiver.

"This is Carolyn," she said. The voice she heard was muffled, difficult to understand, but probably male.

"Two million dollars," it said, "apiece," then the phone went dead. David made the next calls with his cell phone, then waited until his instrument sang its merry little tune.

"A pay phone on U.S. 1," he said. "Titusville."

"That's not far," Carolyn said. "Maybe forty minutes away."

"The police are already cruising the area, looking for a man and two young boys."

~~~~~~~~~~~

Sly had discovered more than one way to keep the boys quiet. In addition to ice cream, they liked peanut butter and jelly sandwiches, chocolate cake, and pizza. Best of all, they loved to ride on his motorcycle.

After he made the call, Sly wheeled back onto the highway holding Timmy and Andrew in front of him. They shrieked with joy as he tore down the back roads of North Merritt Island. What he was unwilling to admit even to himself was the growing pleasure working its way into his psyche, a gift from the little boys.

Their excitement renewed a long-dead and simple joy, a feeling he'd not experienced since childhood. He rode around for an hour, taking them far from the phone he'd used to call Carolyn.

On the eastern edge of Orlando, he spotted a clothing resale shop on Old Colony Drive. He held a tired and therefore quiet boy in each arm when he entered. Comfortable with its musty smells, over-filled tables, and dim lighting, Sly greeted the very large woman who sat behind the counter.

"We're looking for party costumes," he said. "I'm thinking of little girls dress-up clothes and maybe some strings of beads." She pointed to a table near the door.

"That's as good as it gets anywhere. I suppose they want high heeled shoes. We could do witches or ghosts or cowboys, if they'd like that better." She eyed the boys. "I'd say about a size five or six." She waddled over to help him choose.

Sly added a pink baseball cap for each boy and tucked the four costumes into his saddle pack. Two Happy Meals later, he headed eastward. The sky had begun to darken, making his cargo of children nearly invisible. Later the boys fell asleep watching a movie.

Tomorrow we move and paint the truck, he promised himself. He wanted to get across several state lines, but how could he pick up the ransom money he needed from the backwoods of West Virginia?

CHAPTER 12

Thursday, July 17th

"I'm afraid my milk is drying up," Martha said. She had held herself together by feverishly hovering over Susan. Reacting to her mother's anxiety, the baby grew progressively fussier. "I'll run out to buy some cans of formula and nursing bottles, but I'm taking her with me."

She'd notified Lucas, and he'd arranged for emergency leave. He could be in Florida as early as the following morning. David made a deal with her airline, getting her an indefinite delay for her return flight to Des Moines.

"We'll stick here by the phone," David said. "Everything will be fine." He kept busy coordinating the actions of the local police with FBI. The elevator buttons hadn't yielded any fingerprints clear enough to identify the boys' captor, but the disappearance of Sly at the same time the boys vanished made him a prime suspect. Linda's officers found the Harley strewn about in dozens of greasy parts on the floor of his garage. However, a second motorcycle registered to him had turned up in a search of Florida records. They now sought a blue

Kawasaki with a black flame design on the gas tank as well as an enclosed truck.

~~~~~~~~~~~

"The boys don't have helmets. I hope they're not riding with him on a motorcycle," Carolyn said. "They could be killed." David knew that should be the least of her worries, and so did she. She had cancelled her classes for the rest of the week. After her drawings and photographs of the boys were out to news channels and police in Florida and surrounding states, there was little for her to do. She waited in her dad's unit, tethered to the phone, filled with anguish yet fighting to maintain hope. David reached across the small kitchen table for her hand.

"There's been no sign of the cycle or the truck and we don't know that Sly has the boys," he said.

"Linda wormed some information out of Byron," Carolyn said. "Sly was in our building yesterday. He and Byron had another argument. Byron said he left shortly before he heard the police sirens."

"Left in what? We haven't found anybody who saw Sly's truck, a blue cycle, or Sly with the boys." Carolyn stood and walked to the window.

"Not only that, but we have nowhere near four million dollars. I keep looking for the FEDEX man. He's supposed to bring an overnight check from my trust account."

"Your grandfather was a generous man." Carolyn drummed her fingers on the window sill.

"I'll have to deposit it before three o'clock. Thank God my bank's main office approved issuing the cash without the usual three day waiting period."

"Donations are pouring in from all over the country, mostly in cash."

"The kid's pictures are so sweet, and Andrew's dad being
~~~~~~~~~~~

off in Iraq adds to the pathos," Carolyn said. "We couldn't ask for better news coverage, and with all the National Guard members gathering funds . . ." David looked glum.

"Ransom payments seldom work out." He didn't want to expand on this opinion. "Besides, we haven't had any information about a drop."

"If we get our boys back, I swear I'll be good for the rest of my life. I'll tithe; I'll go to church every Sunday; I'll . . . " The phone rang. Carolyn picked it up, and David listened on the extension.

"Got the cash?" the voice asked. David nodded.

"Yes," she said.

"Alligator Bar and Grill on west 520 at the St. John's. Got it?"

"Yes."

"Eleven-thirty tonight. In the back." The caller hung up. Carolyn flung herself into David' arms.

"Oh, God! What will I do?"

~~~~~~~~~~~

Tears streamed down Martha's face when they told her of the meeting. She clutched Susan who'd just wakened from a nap. The baby squirmed to get loose then burst into sobs of her own. The phone rang, this time for David. He listened, put down the receiver, and reported to his sister and Carolyn.

"Sly's truck was parked in a campground on U.S. 1 for the past three nights. He'd rigged up an air conditioner to cool it, but he left early this morning. No one was up to notice the direction it took. No one saw two little boys, but the detectives found ice cream cone wrappers and pizza boxes in the trash. They're checking now for prints."

"Let's gather the funds we have."

"I've emptied out that's available in my account," Carolyn said. "Dad wired fifty thousand, that's all he could get on such
~~~~~~~~~~~

short notice. I pawned my grandmother's gold chains for a few hundred more."

"My folks came up with thirty thousand," Martha said. "They could raise more on the house and investments, but that would take time."

"The problem is making sure we get the boys, not in giving away money," David said. It was easy to agree with FBI policy against payment of ransom when you read it in a manual but more difficult to apply to your own nephew and Carolyn's Timmy.

"David, I don't care what it costs. I'm not willing to take chances," Martha said.

"We'll use my gym bag," Carolyn said. "It's gray, floppy, and holds a lot."

"There'll be a tracker in it, but don't stuff in extra paper. What we have is what he gets." Against all FBI regs, David had kicked in his bank account to the bottom dollar. Damn Mia! If she hadn't nearly cleaned him out before she left, he'd have more for this emergency.

"We'll both drive," Carolyn said. "I know that bar. The road behind it wanders along the banks of the St. John's River. Very curvy, but there's a fence. We could trap Sly with two cars."

"First, we get the boys, then we worry about catching Sly. You're not to frighten him in any way until Andrew and Timmy are safe. And, Martha, don't even think about taking your gun."

~~~~~~~~~~

Sly had been very careful not to be seen with both boys together in the campground, but he figured it was time to move along. Find something more private. He visualized a spot at the end of a lane and off of paved roads. There were hundreds of lakes in Florida; no, more like thousands. There'd be dirt lanes used by fishermen and hunters. That's what he needed. He'd
~~~~~~~~~~

have to do without electricity, but he'd have privacy. Lake Washington was too busy, but there were other choices.

The boys thought it was fun to dress up like dancers. Didn't they see that on TV all the time? So if anyone looked into the truck while he was driving, they'd see two little girls. Their shouts and squeals made the corners of his mouth turn up. Two cute kids. Good natured, too. Fortunately, they were too young to identify him or tell about where they'd been.

The St. John's River had pontoon boats, air boats, canoes, fishing boats but too much traffic. It picked up deeper-hulled power boats and houseboats as it flowed north past De Losandro. There was a stretch hard to access north of 520, but there weren't enough trees. He needed to be in the back country southwest of Palm Shores Retreat where most of the land was occupied by herons, ibises, and wood storks. That's what he needed, remoteness and privacy.

Something clicked. Houseboats! Snag a houseboat. That way he could be mobile yet have access to everything he needed. He swung onto the ramp for I-95. Plenty of those at the marina on Wood Stork Lake. He could jump an engine as well as anybody, but hiding his truck would be difficult. They still had to paint it and change the plates. So he needed paint, brushes, and some food. He knew just the place to get it all. The store would be too busy mid-morning for anyone to notice him.

He parked between two motor homes, nicely concealed by their mammoth bulk. Others shoppers would avoid the area because of the annoying throb of their generators. All kinds of campers had gotten the idea to spend the night in Wal-Mart parking lots, where they could set up their grills, buy supplies, and chat with other travelers rent free.

Would he be able to get the Kawasaki onto a houseboat? Why not, if he chose the right one. Many had their own dories and davits; if they could hold boats, there should be plenty of room for his bike. He'd grab the ransom and motor up to Jacksonville.

He'd never had enough money, but that was about to change.

Maybe one of those giant RVs would be his first big purchase. He could go anywhere, stay anywhere, and move on. No damn shop to open every morning and no whining customers with their pitiful possessions in hand begging him for more cash.

He walked in through the sliding doors, smiled at the greeter, grabbed two sacks of candy off the shelf for the boys, and headed down the aisle.

Total time: less than fifteen minutes for shopping, checking out in the speedy purchase line, and making it through the exit doors. Who would notice a middle-aged man preparing for ordinary household maintenance duties?

He neared the truck and immediately saw that the boys weren't in it. Panic wrapped itself around his chest like the sinewy coils of a boa constrictor. Maybe they were hiding. He opened the door to look.

"Over here," he heard a voice call. "They're safe and sound. My wife's a nut for kids, so don't worry." Sly couldn't prevent the sweat that beaded across his face or the pounding of his heart, but he tried to slow his breathing as he turned toward the voice.

A blue-striped awning extended from the motor home's side. On the green outdoor carpeting under the canopy, the two children sat beside a plump, white-haired woman and munched cookies. He knew he shouldn't have left them inside the truck, but taking them into the store would have been even more dangerous.

"They told us all about the party you're having for their mothers and how much they like playing on the beach. Sweet kids. You're the uncle?"

"Right." Sly stood frozen to the pavement. What if they refused to come? What if they started to cry, to beg for their mothers?

"Run along, now," the woman said. "It's been a pleasure to meet you, but I know you have to get ready for your party. Here, take an extra cookie for your uncle."

~~~~~~~~~~~

The shiny metal side panels of the truck didn't take well to the enamel. It slid around like the disparate parts of a bad dream. The boys painted blades of grass along the bottom edge of the box, while he rolled pale blue onto the panels above them. Later he'd fill in palm and orange trees. The boys were soon dotted with green and blue globs of paint. When they tired of their chore, they wandered toward the nearby lake. Maybe it would be nice to be rid of them, but not quite yet.

He dragged them back with the promise of another ride on the cycle. Sly congratulated himself on finding an entirely deserted back road and a little open glade near the water. It was dark and nearly time to head for the Alligator Bar when he finished the paint job. Mosquitoes, moths, flies, and a very large walking stick had affixed themselves to the paint, but nobody, absolutely nobody, would recognize the truck as the one owned by Sly Poltron.

Lacking electricity, they'd have to eat the pizza cold or settle for PBJ's. The boys ate while Sly chugged down a warm beer he found in the corner of the nearly empty refrigerator. The care of children was wearing thin but it would soon be over and he'd be rich enough to find any number of more suitable companions. As he drove to the marina, he dreamed of Vegas, hearing the click of thrown dice and the clink of ice in a glass.

Plenty of action there. It was high time to blow this island and get himself onto a solid piece of mainland.

~~~~~~~~~~~

When the blue Kawasaki coasted past the Alligator Grill, the boys no longer rode in front of Sly. He guessed Carolyn had to be the one with the money from the scene he saw sharply illumined by his headlamp. She stood beside her silly conch car dangling her gym bag casually over a shoulder, as relaxed and unafraid as if her Timmy had been kidnapped every day. He revved his engine and pulled up beside her.

"Where are the little darlings?" she asked, with satin and honey spread liberally across each word. Standing beside Carolyn, Martha stared at him with eyes as round as Frisbees. She was nearly panting. God, he'd never had this effect on women before. It took some effort to keep his plan in focus.

"I'll count the money, then you get the kids," he said.

"We get the children back safely, or no money." Now there was a bit of steel in her voice, and her knuckles whitened with pressure on the handle of the booty bag. He should grab it and make a run for safety.

But where was that federal boy? He hadn't seen any police when he'd checked the place out earlier, and no car had arrived during the hour he'd been watching from behind the billboard. The women wouldn't come alone. Did they think they were dealing with an idiot? Should he risk looking behind? No. He kept his eyes on Carolyn, but the back of his neck prickled with fear. Was there a sharpshooter a few hundred yards away with his head in the sights? Would he pop like a dropped melon?

"Easy, honey. Everything is cool. Drop the bag at your feet and move away."

She did not stir.

Sly allowed his eyes to follow the curve of Carolyn's body upward from the painted toenails, over the long slender legs with one knee bent toward him, and the hip above it pushed lustfully in his direction. They lingered over the shape of her crotch outlined by the clingy material of her dress, then dwelt on the curve of her breasts. He felt pleasure tightening in his groin. At last he took in her pouty lips and half-closed, smoldering eyes.

"On second thought, come with me," he whispered. "We'd have plenty of money and no strings on where we went." Carolyn smiled and turned her head away. Sly did not see the wink she gave Martha but he did pick up on the slight narrowing of Martha's eyes. The resulting flicker of doubt did not reach from his brain far enough into his body to effect his swelling arousal.

"Anything you want, just get me to Timmy," Carolyn said, returning her gaze to Sly. She tossed her car keys to Martha and leaned over the Kawasaki. She slammed the bag into its travel bin and hopped on behind him. A surprised Sly understood then that Carolyn knew her way around a motorcycle. She grabbed the passenger strap as Sly jerked the machine forward. He roared off past the restaurant, past the cars parked near it, and onto the four lane highway.

Sly rode with skill and precision, out of habit, but his mind foamed and frothed. Why had he succumbed to her lure? Was it those long legs stretching out beneath her mini-skirt, the breasts nearly spilling from her impossibly scanty top, or the fragility of the spaghetti straps over her shoulders? God! What should he do now?

He couldn't head for the truck. He'd locked the boys up where they'd never be found, but where could he take Carolyn and the money? Damn!

He'd made a plan and then dumped it the minute Carolyn gave him that come-on pose.

He needed a new plan, and fast. He didn't see any headlights that looked like a tail. A motel. That's what he needed. A room, a bed, a hot shower. It would feel so good . . . then there was Carolyn, pleading for Timmy. At last he had something she wanted—her son. Now he could most certainly get himself what he'd craved since sixth grade.

~~~~~~~~~~~

David watched from the mildewy weeds at the edge of the marshland. He must be lying in leeches. Water had seeped into his hip boots and soaked his socks and underwear. He was a living, breathing piece of alligator bait. Even so, nothing in the past hours or days could have prepared him for watching Carolyn leap onto the cycle behind Sly and disappear into the darkness.

Was everything that happened a plot to dupe him? Was he the stranger taken in by the wiles of the home boys? Carolyn and Sly had gone through school together. He could be some nonsensical part of their plan to get thousands of dollars. He waded onto the bank and stumbled toward his sister.

"Jesus, Martha. What happened?" David wanted to shake her and strangle Carolyn. She'd done nothing he asked of her and everything he hadn't.

"She'll be okay. She has the tracker and my gun."

"Your gun!" He thought of the thin dress she wore. "Where in the hell could she stash a gun? She's roaring around on a cycle with no helmet and no boots. What an idiot!" Martha's look was full of pity, but she opened the door of the little conch car and lowered herself into the driver's seat.

"We didn't think your plan was any better. Now will you please lead off so I can follow? You have the scanner to keep track of her and I don't."
~~~~~~~~~~~

CHAPTER 13

Sweat beaded on Carolyn's skin in the muggy night air as she waited for Sly, but the chilling wind of the high-speed motorcycle ride soon dried her off. A cold numbness worked its way from her fingertips and toes toward the center of her body. Even Sly's muscled width and a wide windscreen failed to keep moths, gnats, and mosquitoes from mashing themselves on her. She leaned her head into his back and pulled closer, hoping for a little protection. How long could her fingers hold on? Would her idea work? Were the boys even still alive?

It just wasn't possible that she had gotten herself entangled with her high-school nemesis.

Sly liked the feel of Carolyn behind him, liked balancing the extra weight. He did a small wheelie as he left the next stop light and worried he might throw her off. He slowed to fifty, but he still felt like a kid, a cocky kid who'd not yet had four wives leave him and hadn't mortgaged his business beyond recovery.

The money. How was he to gain control of the money, return the boys to their mothers, and get away to Vegas without being arrested? Was that why so few kidnap victims came back alive?

He ran several motels through his head, then remembered the self-registration units on the beach. Stick in your credit card and pull out a key. Off season there'd be empty units and no desk clerk to ask questions or check his license plate. A string of car lights reflected in his rear view mirror, but he didn't see the uniquely low, round pair of headlamps that distinguished Carolyn's conch mobile. Where was his tail?

~~~~~~~~~~~

Carolyn realized with shock that Sly rode east toward Sunny Shores. She thrilled as the bike took them up over the causeway bridge and down into her home town. Were the boys here? She couldn't ask herself if they were safe. They had to be.

He hesitated at the off-ramp for the south port road but swerved left onto the main highway. Had he returned the boys to the condominium? Maybe they were tucked into bed, asleep in her dad's unit. The thought filled her with hope, but when Sly veered sharply into the parking lot of a darkened motel, it hit her.

He wasn't taking her to the boys at all. He was taking her to bed. Her vamping to distract him had backfired. Her throat constricted as he pulled to a stop.

"Off," he ordered. Her legs wouldn't move, stiff as they were with cold and fear. Sly threw his arm around her waist and dragged her from the rear seat. She wanted to drop to the ground and curl up in a fetal ball but she forced her legs to hold her up. She wanted to kick him, pound his face senseless, take out the little pistol and shoot him. At such close range, a shot between the eyes would certainly do the job.

But no, first she had to find Timmy and Andrew.

Sly rolled the bike to a spot between two pickup trucks. He grabbed the little satchel from the carrier with one hand and Carolyn's arm with the other. She'd never seen him so revved,
~~~~~~~~~~~

so sure of himself, so repulsive. Don't show your disgust, she admonished herself. Smile. Look seductive. Look conquered. God! Why had she quit the drama club in tenth grade?

"I'm sure you have a sexy little nightie in here and you wrapped the cash in lacy black underwear?" He wriggled his eyebrows and grinned, Groucho style. Is he mad? Doesn't he understand I'm frantic with worry about Timmy? She widened her eyes. Maybe I'm the crazy one.

A well-lit metal rack of key boxes hung on the wall inside a small covered passage. No longer chilled by wind, Carolyn's skin drank in the warmth of the night, reveled in the familiar generosity of the onshore breeze. She breathed in the tangy odors of the sea, nutrition for her weakened spirit.

Sly tucked the satchel up under his arm and shoved his credit card into a slot. A box opened. He removed a key, never releasing her hand. Where did he think she'd go without Timmy? Nevertheless, it was nice to know he harbored a bit of anxiety. Maybe it would put him off guard enough so that she could learn where he'd left the boys.

Keep away, David, she silently ordered. Let me handle this. He'd know exactly where she stood and where the bag went, maybe even saw the two of them under the porch light, but he should stand off.

~~~~~~~~~~~

David stayed well behind the Kawasaki. He dreaded the thought of finding a broken Carolyn lying beside the highway; he kept his lights on high. What was she thinking, riding with Sly with nothing but a thin dress to protect her from vicious scrapes and broken bones? Were the boys safe, and where were they?

The only lead he'd gotten came from a Speedway east of the St. John's River. Sly had filled both the truck's gas tank and the
~~~~~~~~~~~

Kawasaki's and been foolish enough to pay for the gas with his credit card. The county sheriff had his full complement of deputies out searching all the back roads within ten miles of the gas station. Teams of volunteers from the local National Guard unit expanded the number of men and women on the hunt for the two kidnapped boys.

Bless Chief Linda! She had ordered a cast made of the tires tracks behind Sly's pawn shop before it rained, and given each team a photocopy of the tread pattern of his truck. They checked dirt roads with spotlights, but even so, tracks would be hard to spot in the dark. Daylight was hours away. Were the boys tied up? Hidden in a box? Or buried? Or drowned?

David knew nothing of the web of fishing trails that ran off the few paved roads in the unpopulated areas west of I-95, but Sly did, and it was Sly they followed. He and Martha drove past the motel that harbored Carolyn and parked both cars across the highway in front of an all-night deli. David jumped from his car.

"Damn!" he said, his head poking through her window. "We couldn't search every motel in the county."

It was unlikely Sly had brought Carolyn to the boys. Linda said he wasn't too bright, but even an idiot wouldn't walk into certain capture. David watched the couple walk through the small portico and pass into the unlit darkness beyond. He heard a door open, then close. His skin crawled; he pounded his fist against the car roof as he fought for control.

Bashing in on them wouldn't be a good idea, but it was the only satisfactory action that came to mind. He leaned against Carolyn's car, hoping his heart wouldn't pop from the pounding, rushing, boiling flow of blood through it.

His sister sat behind the wheel, cramped for leg room and stiff with worry. Carolyn had a good plan, but Sly was a loose cannon. Martha watched David grab for his cell phone, watched him listen and smile, then saw his face sag with disappointment.

"The National Guard volunteers located a spot where Sly's truck has been, found empty paint cans, splattered paint, trampled grass, refuse . . ."

"But the truck is gone," Martha said, "along with the boys. I knew they'd be too late. I've been too late ever since the elevator went up without me." David tried to comfort her, patting her arm, but she jerked away.

"The guardsmen will check a wider area," he said, "when we get daylight, but for now . . . "

"There's nothing they can do for now." Her voice was grim and certain.

"Not so. They're searching in small grids, half a mile in all directions. Remember night vision goggles? If the boys are there, they'll find them."

"If they're alive. Sly has the money; why should he keep them safe?"

David opened the car door and pulled his sister out.

"Mom and Dad will be here by noon tomorrow." He tried to calm her with a reassuring voice.

"They can help with Susan. I've got to think of Susan." David felt her stiffen in his arms, as if trying to dig up the resolution to continue life without Andrew.

"Andrew will be fine. The boys were in good shape this morning when a couple of tourists talked to them in the Wal-Mart parking lot.

"You didn't tell me about that!" Martha shrieked.

"The woman fed them cookies. Said they talked to her nicely and performed somersaults on her carpet. The couple didn't see the story on TV until evening, and even then it took awhile for them to realize the girls she'd fed cookies to were our missing boys. She's distraught about letting Sly take them away."

Even that message of hope failed to lighten Martha's load of fears. "We're always too late. Too late," she said.

"What's Carolyn up to?" He wanted to shake his sister,

squeeze her to make the truth pop out. What was happening behind the closed door of that motel room?

"She made me promise not to tell."

"I can guess and you can nod or shake your head. Is she seducing Sly?" The thought of Sly's white hands on Carolyn snarled in his gut.

"That's a silly child's game." Martha shook her head.

"Maybe it's a game that will lead us to Andrew and Timmy." Martha turned away. They stood by the deli and waited, soaked in futility and drenched in loss. David struggled against the gnarled cords of indecision even as he tried to comfort Martha.

In the end, caution and discipline gave way to his natural bent for action. Carolyn had been all too clear about not wanting him to interfere, but he raced across the street and around to the back of the motel.

Old, and built as a continuous two-story structure, each apartment boasted sliding glass doors and a continuous deck overlooking the ocean. He stopped beneath the only unit with lights on, the one the hand-held GPS tracker showed as the location of the bag and the money.

No more deaths, he told himself. There had been enough bodies on this beach. Damn. They were on the second floor. Where were the stairs?

Martha beckoned from the end of the building beside the steps.

"Wait!" David whispered. "There's an alarm system." It took agonizing minutes to bypass a connection so they could climb over the locked gate and make their way quietly to the upper level. The curtains of the lighted unit had been pulled shut. He needed to find an opening, but the voices that came through the receiver bug told too much.

Sly was counting the money.

"Not enough," he yelled. "You're cheating me. Stupid bitch!" Dangerous anger poured out of the speaker and pummeled the inside of David's skull.

"It's all we had, Sly. Take it and go. I promise you won't be followed. Just tell me where the boys are. Please. You're a good person. You don't want them to be hurt."

"You're going along. We'll get more money. Two kids and you. That's worth twice as much."

"Sly, it won't work. Give it up. Let us help you get out of whatever trouble you're in. You're making matters worse every minute you hold the children." Her voice crackled through the air waves with an old-time tininess.

"I know," he said. "It was a mistake. Everything was a mistake." David felt the sourness of Sly's defeat and a hint of pity tickled the back of his brain.

"Don't make it worse." Her voice became soft, seductive. "Give up. Linda will help you any way she can. David will, too. Just give it up." A pause. Then she gasped.

~~~~~~~~~~~

Sly's shoulders drew back, his mouth dropped open, his eyes bulged.

"What's that lump in the front of your dress?" he yelled. "You growing a third breast?" At the rush of quick movement and Carolyn's scream, David shot into the lock on the sliding glass doors. He yanked with all his strength

Martha pointed to the metal bar blocking the slide of the inner panel.

Carolyn screamed again as a thundering shot echoed through the stillness of the night like an order to advance. David pounded on the door with the butt of his gun. Thank God the glass was old and brittle.

He shoved Martha aside so the concrete block walls of the motel would shield her from bullets, but he himself stepped through the broken glass into the room.

Carolyn's hand reached out to David before she fell into his
~~~~~~~~~~~

arms. Blood streaked her face, dripped from her forehead, and smeared her dress.

Lights came on in the other units, heads poked out of doors—someone nearby called for the police. Sly stood in the middle of the room, pointing Martha's gun at Carolyn.

"I couldn't do it," she said. "I couldn't." David handed his cell phone to Martha.

"Don't make that call," Sly pleaded, his voice a hoarse whisper.

"Where is Timmy," Martha hissed. "Where did you put my Andrew?" Sly's eyes glazed over; his lips struggled to form words. Puffy and white, they no longer sneered but took on the seriousness of intense effort; he tried to answer.

"Marina," he croaked. "Boat."

His eyes rolled upward; he crumpled forward and fell onto the floor at their feet. As Carolyn gagged and retched into the bathroom sink, Martha reached the 911 operator. Speaking with a precise and calm voice, she described the two who needed emergency treatment and gave the correct address. David led Carolyn out to the courtyard fountain. She knelt by the low wall and splashed cool water onto her face. He took off his shirt so she could use it to dry herself. She straightened her shoulders and sat beside him.

"I want to run into the ocean and never turn around," she said. "I am so filthy."

"I'll go with you," David said. "We will come back together."

"Not for what I did. For what I intended to do."

"We have to find the boys."

"I worked myself up to seduce him. I would be clever, I would get him in my power," Carolyn sobbed. "I would do anything."

"There must be fifty marinas in this county alone, with a hundred boats in each. The river, the lakes, the inland waterway."

"Sly wouldn't tell me where . . . the boys may already be . . . Oh, God!" She buried her face in her hands, leaned forward, and pressed them against her knees.

"We'll find them," he said, pulling her close. "Everybody is hunting. National Guard, police, countless citizens. Now we can be more specific in our search."

"Sly can't tell us anything with that bullet in his brain. I thought I could do anything, but the blast of blood flew into my face . . . all over me."

Friday, July 18th

Linda and David contacted every police department in a radius of forty miles. Carolyn sat in Linda's office at the station, her face pale, leaning her head against the wall behind her.

"Search all marina parking lots in your area," she heard her sister say. "We're faxing you the dimensions of the truck, a description of the cab, and a copy of the tire tread pattern. It's been newly painted with blue and green enamel, design unknown."

Working from the south end of Sunny Shores to the north, it took hours for Linda's officers to locate Sly's truck. He'd parked between two tour busses in a remote corner of a county park and marina. The team spent more anxious minutes prying open the rear door, minutes made to seem like hours because of the silence from within. They moved every piece of furniture, opened every box.

No boys, no body parts, thank God!, and not even a single child's toy or game.

David, Martha, and Carolyn arrived at the Scalina Marina shortly after they began a systematic search of the boats moored in the basin.

"They must be nearby, somewhere in this maze of piers," Carolyn said. David eyed the array of tall-masted sailing ships, deep-hulled sport fishing boats with a dozen poles and antennae on each, shorter ski boats, squat houseboats, and rusty, well-used commercial shrimp boats. The array of water craft stretched out for blocks, tied up on both sides of narrow wooden piers. Did one of the eerily creaking boats hold two poisoned children?

"The marina staff is searching all boats from A1 through to the last slip," Linda said. "See? Each of them carries a pail of keys. They'll inspect every craft."

"It's taking too long. Are you sure they're really here?" Martha ran onto the first pier. "Timmy, Andrew! It's Mommy. You're safe," she called. "Mommy's here." Her voice quavered as she choked back sobs. Carolyn and David raced between another row of boats, crying the same message.

The staff searched through the boats at slips numbered in the thirties, the forties, the fifties. The minutes dragged. Martha and Carolyn raced up and down the wobbly docks, calling for their boys. The sun had risen, blasting the temperature into the high nineties. How dangerous for the boys shut up in a sweltering cuddy!

At last an officer emerged from the cabin of the boat at 57E and waved a handkerchief over his head. "Over here," he yelled, and he dived back through the narrow cabin door.

It took agonizing seconds for the three to race back to shore and down the length dock E. Carolyn reached the boat first, leapt onto the deck and received a limp, red-faced Timmy into her arms. The dock boy emerged next carrying Andrew.

"Water!" he shouted. "Get these kids something to drink!"

~~~~~~~~~~~

Inside the marina office, chilled Gator Ade became a healing elixir. Each boy snuggled into his mother's arms, passive, dazed, sipping through a straw. Carolyn rocked Timmy, her eyes soft
~~~~~~~~~~~

and brimming with love. Tears streamed down her face, unnoticed; she didn't bother to wipe them away. Martha's eyes were clamped shut. She sobbed quietly and held her son as if she'd never let him go.

"Should we have them checked at the hospital?" Carolyn asked. David nodded.

"Yes. They were in that hot cabin for hours and could have fevers, but we won't need the National Guard truck and ambulance that just pulled up in front. The boys can ride in one of our cars." Andrew suddenly darted from his mother's arms and ran to the glass entry doors.

"Daddy!" he called. "Daddy!" A tall soldier scooped him up and planted hungry kisses all over his sweaty little face. Martha jumped up and ran to Lucas, holding father and son in her arms. They swayed together and cried. There wasn't a dry eye in the room.

A burly, gray-haired man entered through the dock-side doors, hesitated, and walked to the service counter where a matronly blonde clerk wept openly.

"You called. Is something wrong with my boat? What's going on here?"

"We need to have you check it over," the woman said, wiping the back of her hand across her eyes. "Someone broke into it last night and stowed those two children in your cabin." She pointed in the direction of Andrew and Timmy, smiled, and dabbed again at her tears.

"Not the two kidnapped children?"

"The very ones." The man turned pale.

"Are they all right?"

"We think so," Carolyn said, "but they might have broken something before they were tied up."

"Thank God! The boat can be repaired, but you've had everybody in the state down on their knees. My wife's even doing a novena and fasting. There will be tears of joy from one end of Florida to the other." He shook hands with both boys and congratulated their parents. Tears watered his own eyes as he headed outside.

The next person to burst into the Marina office had short orange hair gelled upward into jagged peaks and carried a camera.

"I'm from *Florida Today*," she said. She snapped a picture of Lucas holding Andrew before anyone could stop her and turned the camera on Carolyn and Timmy, whose triumphant smile gave the reporter a prize-winning photo.

It was the accidental inclusion of David standing protectively behind them with his arms around both that enraged Allison Granby.

CHAPTER 14

Saturday, July 19th

Allison studied the front page of the morning paper. First she examined the top picture of a man being wheeled away on a gurney, his face hidden behind an oxygen mask. Likely he wasn't dead if the medics hadn't covered his face or zipped him into a body bag. Nevertheless, the headline screamed of Professor Carolyn Brockton's vengeful shooting of the kidnapper during a lover's tryst.

But it was the lower picture that made her gag. Timmy and that impossibly stupid artist! It should have been Allison herself holding him, Allison in the arms of the sexy FBI agent, and Allison on the front page of the newspaper.

If the kidnapper died and Carolyn went to prison for murder, she could get Timmy back. Is that what she wanted?

No, something better. What would Carolyn pay to keep him?

A lawsuit. That was it. She could think of no better solution. She'd file a petition claiming Carolyn hadn't adequately cared for Timmy and had allowed him to experience irreparable emotional damage; then she'd settle for big bucks to drop the case.

Allison looked around her tiny kitchen at the small, green refrigerator left over from the sixties and the gas stove with crud-covered burners and filthy drip pans. The flowered curtains she'd bought at the Dollar Store failed to hide the greasy film on the windows behind them. Everything would be perfect if she had the money to hire a cleaning crew. No, she needed a much better place to live.

~~~~~~~~~~~

In Leighton Scott's reception area, she read and reread the story. Even so, she found her excitement calmed by the serene arrangement of two paisley-covered wing chairs, a classic cherry tray-table, and subdued impressionist prints on the walls. Her breathing and pulse rates had nearly returned to normal by the time the receptionist beckoned.

"Mr. Scott will see you now." The girl wore a sleek black skirt wrapped around her very slim hips. A black-and-white silk blouse stretched across the nubile swelling of her breasts. Allison Granby's eyes traveled from the disciplined French roll and gold clip at the back of the girl's head to her gleaming patent leather sandals. The outfit cost more than Allison's entire wardrobe. Size four, no doubt.

She followed the narrow hips into the office of the attorney whose name appeared at the top of the firm's gold-lettered stationery.

He was the rainmaker and never handled the *pro bono* cases the bar association sent his firm; younger and more recent graduates did that financially unrewarding work.

How fortunate that she'd found a part-time job as a receptionist for the Escaneda County Bar Association. Allison debated that morning about which attorney to contact. Should she pick a young one eager to gain clients or an experienced lawyer with political clout? As she walked down the hall, she
~~~~~~~~~~~

rehearsed her cause. She wanted what was rightfully hers: Timmy. There had to be a way. She was just as pretty as Carolyn, and younger, too. She was the real mother.

It wasn't fair that Carolyn had both the child and the handsome hero. Worst of all, she had her picture on the front page of the newspaper.

When Allison finished law school next June, she'd have not only the top grades in her class, but she'd also have a well-known name. She'd be the most envied graduate at the reception, having been given the best job in her graduating class.

She struggled to bring herself back to the present as the attorney spoke. He'd actually risen from his chair as she entered and leaned over to shake her hand. Wasn't that nice! How tall he was, how dignified.

"Good morning, Miss Granby. Please take a chair." Allison settled her size sixteen hips onto the leather cushion of the wing chair across from Mr. Leighton Scott. She smiled at him, revealing deep and often-used dimples.

"Has your office taken to hand-delivering the cases you want us to accept?" he asked. Her smile flattened as she felt a flush wash across her skin.

"Not at all. This is a personal matter." Mr. Scott tapped the pad of paper with a fat gold pen. A Cross pen, she thought. How these big boys do show off! With that one gesture, he became her enemy. She felt her bile rise. It was suddenly wrong to be here asking for help. His silver hair was much too perfectly groomed and his tan too dramatic against his white teeth.

"I want my son back," she began. Ten minutes later, she could say one thing about Mr. Scott: he listened. He also made notes. When she wound down, his questions were few and technical.

"You're sure the father was properly notified?"

"Certainly. Published exactly according to legal requirements for notice." Allison found herself nodding her head vigorously.

"I'm talking about personal notification. Did you tell the man of your pregnancy and of his son's birth?"

"I did not, but he was long gone. A sailor in port for the commissioning of his ship. We met on a Caribbean cruise. One look at Timmy and you know what a cute guy he was." She shoved the boy's photograph part way across the width of Mr. Scott's desk. "I've no idea where the father is."

"We need to be absolutely sure of your rights in order to break the adoption. You have entirely followed the court's decision?" Allison nodded and smiled. "I've visited Timmy at least once a month, according our agreement."

"It's easy to trace our country's enlisted men. If the government does nothing else well, it keeps track of its personnel. What is the sailor's name?" Allison stared at the pen poised over his yellow legal pad. Why was he digging into this buried pain? There was no handsome sailor in port and no beach meeting.

The truth was, she'd seduced the sixteen-year old brother of a child she baby-sat while their parents took a cruise.

"I don't know. You know how these things are. First names in the dark, passionate moments."

"Dancing in the moonlight, champagne, sex on deck in the rising swells of the Caribbean—that sort of romantic thing?" The attorney's chiseled features remained in place, his expression unreadable. She felt reassured; her secret was safe, but then he added, "What else are you not telling me?"

The hot lead of shock poured through Allison. Her story had been accepted by the attorney who handled the adoption; why didn't Mr. Fancy-name Scott believe her?

"What is it you're really after, Miss Granby, and why now?"

"I don't understand," she said.

"Miss Granby, I served a hitch in the Navy. You don't find United States sailors wandering about on a cruise liner. You need clean hands to succeed in this matter. I suspect, at least as far as this case goes, that yours are not." Allison hefted herself out of her chair and walked toward the door. He ripped his sheet of notes from the yellow pad.

"I'll assign your case to Stephanie Glazer. She's very good and has an excellent record in the family law division. Please see the receptionist for an appointment." He stood, walked around his desk, and shook her hand. "You'll do well. Grace under pressure, determination, and all that sort of thing. Good luck; and by the way, the advance payment will be a thousand dollars."

~~~~~~~~~~~

Things had not gone according to her plan. She fumed and pounded on the steering wheel all the way back to her apartment. The arrogant prick! She knew just where she wanted his gold pen painfully stuffed.

Allison Granby did not come close to having a thousand dollars. Every extra cent she earned went for law books. Well, nearly every cent. Occasionally she sipped on a Cappuccino Smoothie. Beer came free, scrounged at local bars from men who would buy a drink for anything in a skirt. The scholarship she'd won paid her tuition, but books were another matter. This, the summer before her third year of law school, she studied nearly all the time for her night classes. She was sick of the all-work, no-play. With a hunk of money from Carolyn, she could quit her job, get a better apartment, and pay for a weight-loss program.

She didn't want to hear snickers behind her as she stood before the judge's bench. A size twelve wouldn't be so bad and new clothes would help immensely. Allison headed for the law library. She'd locate the proper forms and do this case herself. Civil procedures were a pain, but hadn't she just gotten an A in the course? One of her many A's?
~~~~~~~~~~~

~~~~~~~~~~~

By the time Carolyn saw the Petition to Void the Adoption of a Minor, Sly had been moved from the hospital to a county jail cell, Martha had flown back to Iowa with her two children, Lucas had returned to Iraq, and David was on the job in Kansas City.

Carolyn's first impulses raced across her mind like the fast-forwarded credits on a rental movie.

Hire a lawyer.

Take Timmy away from Florida.

Ignore the papers.

Pay her off.

That was it! Allison wanted money. The girl barely spent fifteen minutes of the monthly hour she was entitled to have with Timmy; she didn't want the care of a child. This had to be about money. What about the ransom money she'd gotten back from Sly? She'd give it to Allison. She reached for her phone even as it rang.

"Doctor Brockton's office," she announced, then laughed. "Yes, it's Carolyn. I was just calling you. Did you get a psychic message?" She stood and walked toward the easel set up in the corner of her book-lined office.

"No, no. I didn't say sexual, I said psychic." She looked up from the painting to study the administration building across the campus drive.

"What's going on is that I'm being blackmailed by Timmy's birth mother. I told you about Allison." Carolyn paused to listen.

"Not in so many words, but I'm convinced money is behind her petition. I'll FAX you a copy. Please tell me what you think." She fingered a paintbrush.

"She claims I've put her son in harm's way, and she wants him back." Carolyn nodded and picked up a dab of paint on the tip of the brush.
~~~~~~~~~~~

"Yes, you're right, I'm sure," David said.

"Right now, I need to curl up on your lap and be soothed like a colicky infant. What I'll do instead is lose myself in painting."

"I'll catch the red eye tonight," he said.

"Thank you for offering to come, but you have a job in Kansas City. I'm a big girl. I'll survive." She listened, gasped, and then responded with excitement.

"Can you really do that? I mean, isn't it an invasion of privacy?" Pause. "But I'd love it, of course. I'll find some spies around campus, and you find out whatever you can. Two can play at the blackmail game." Pause. "How's everything going with you?"

"My new assistant is working out well. I've gotten to the driving range four times this week. I miss you."

"I miss you, too. I'm working on something to make my bosses happy, a painting of the old red-brick administration building. You should see what I've done to the front portico."

"I always did think of Grecian columns as phallic symbols of masculine domination."

"You guessed it. They do look more like penises than pillars and are definitely large enough to hold up the heavy tile roof."

"Wouldn't it be better on my office wall?" David asked.

"You cannot have this painting. It's destined for bribery." She positioned the receiver between her cheek and shoulder, and dipped a brush into ocher pigment. "I'll be in Kansas City as soon as I get things in order here. What I'm after is a leave of absence, not a resignation." Her frown deepened as she listened.

"Come on David, we don't need to argue about that. What if you get transferred to Florida? I'd want my old position back without a pay or status cut." She reached for her desk and picked up the sheaf of papers, the petition that threatened to take Timmy from her.

"What if I just hauled Timmy off to another state. Yours, for example. Would that work?" Carolyn chewed on a corner of her lower lip.

"That's asking for trouble."

"I knew you'd say that. The light is perfect now for painting. After my three o'clock class I'm going for a run to cool off. What are you doing after work?"

"I'm taking a kid to get glasses. You know, the Big Brother thing. We'll maybe shoot hoops after that. How could a run in afternoon heat cool you off?"

"I know it's hot here, but I'm talking about my internal temperature. Miss Allison's little papers set my blood to boil. Besides, we have an inside track in an air-conditioned gym on campus. Wouldn't you like to become an instructor here, say in criminal justice?"

"Cool off in an attorney's office?"

"That's your final word?"

Carolyn looked at her watch, put Allison's petition on her desk, and flipped through the phone book. Now what was the name of the firm her college roommate had joined?

She made the call, got an appointment, and resumed her careful work on the dusky live oaks surrounding the administration building. All would be well.

Her new mantra came directly from Dame Julian. All would be well.

Maybe she'd take Timmy for a bike ride over on the beach instead of a run. It was nearly time to pick him up from day care. The talk with David had cheered her and the bike ride would delight Timmy. They'd stop at Sonny's for a BBQ dinner. He'd love it. She washed her brushes in the corner sink and grabbed her class notes.

~~~~~~~~~~~
~~~~~~~~~~~

Carolyn and Timmy hadn't been in Sonny's long before Linda slid into their booth.

"What would you give me to get your handsome agent back to Sunny Shores?"

"A big kiss." Carolyn hugged Linda and planted a generous smack on her sister's face. "What's up?"

"Sly's attorney has pretty well proven Sly didn't kill the three females David found, which points the crime back to our own hapless brother." Timmy handed his aunt a French fry. She gobbled it up and pretended to nibble on his fingers. He giggled and balled them into a tight fist behind his back. "We need to find out who really killed them. Sly probably did poison Mr. Worthan, and we can hold him for trial on the kidnapping."

"Sly told me he was broke. Where's he getting the money for an attorney?"

"It seems the jerk has friends after all. One of his ex wives is making big bucks in porno movies."

"There's no accounting for tastes."

"All the evidence pointed to Sly. We found castor beans growing all over his land and traces of it in the lid and under the ring of his kitchen blender. However, he was in California with his ex the week they died and he didn't get back until after the bodies surfaced. We checked with the airlines and the hotel there. He's in the clear."

"That's not possible."

"You're right, which is why we need your David and his goddamn labs." Timmy's eyes gleamed.

"Aunty Linda said a naughty word," he announced. "Make her pay a dime." Linda fished in her pocket and tossed him a quarter.

"Good boy. Keep the change for the next time you catch me." Timmy dipped another French fry in catsup and handed it to Linda, his grin nearly as wide as his face.

"How did you know where to find us?" Carolyn asked.

"This is my town, and don't you forget it. Now go forth and use your charms on Agent David Santorino."

"Use your own. He'll be here this weekend for Timmy's birthday party. I'm supposed to pick up both Dad and David at the Orlando airport Friday evening."

"David may be among the nation's finest, but he'll need more than two days to clear our dear brother. I can't protect Byron from arrest much longer, and he wouldn't be safe in the county jail."

"What do you mean by that? How could he be not safe in jail?"

"You've read the papers. Too many suicides there already. Those county guards just don't watch the prisoners when they should." Timmy looked up from his French fries.

"Aunty Linda, don't cry. I kiss it and make it well." He stood up to hug his aunt and planted a kiss on her cheek.

"All will be well, all will be well, all will be well," Carolyn whispered.

"What's that? Some of your new-age religion stuff?"

"No, its old. Dame Julian of Norwich had her visions in 1373 and wrote her thoughts about them twenty years later. It's as good a mantra now as it was in those treacherous days."

"Maybe so. I could use some good news; we've certainly had more than enough of the other kind."

"Popsie Worthan told me there's a move afoot to change our town's name from 'Sunny Shores' to 'Dead Body Beach.'"

"Only half said in joking. But I've got to run." She touched a finger to her other cheek and turned it toward Timmy.

"One more kiss, sweetie, right there, and all will be well with your Aunty Linda." As she left, Linda waved to a pair of off-duty police officers.

"Thanks," she called. "Glad to know you're keeping my life in order."

CHAPTER 15

Carolyn's e-mail to David left a great deal unsaid: "Chief Linda needs your help in finding the beach killer. She's being pushed into arresting Byron for the three murders. I'm worried about our brother. He's so fragile. I'll meet your plane Friday evening, but please try to get a few extra days here. All my love, Carolyn."

David's responded with a phone call.

"But the kidnapping charges against Sly are a slam dunk," he said. Linda can do some plea bargaining about the bodies and the fingerprints inside the contaminated water filter. He's got to be involved somehow."

Sly's attorney had efficiently curtailed police questioning. Carolyn's affidavit outlined their struggle for the gun and the accidental shooting. Full of gratitude at getting Timmy back unharmed, Carolyn's anger had turned to pity. Her love for Timmy and for David spread itself like honey on everybody around.

"I don't want to hold a grudge," she said. "The boys are fine."

"How much longer do you think they'd have lasted in that hot cabin without brain damage?" David asked.

"What if Sly really didn't kill those women? What if somebody else did and is still threatening the lives of people in Dad's building?"

"With Sly in jail Linda hasn't found any new bodies."

"I guess not, but I nearly killed him. Isn't that enough pain for what he did?"

"Head wounds bleed a lot, but this one did little internal damage. Lucky for him, the gun was moving when it went off."

"I'm the lucky one. Can you imagine actually killing someone?" David's lengthy pause revealed his own demons.

"Yes, Carolyn. I can. I imagine it all the time, and someone in Sunny Shores has proved to be quite capable of murder."

"The autopsy report said the bodies had been frozen. Isn't that odd?"

"It happens. Lots of businesses have large freezer rooms. I'll do some thinking about your brother's position, but I don't see any factual basis for his arrest. Linda is getting too much media pressure to move before the case is ripe."

"She does not want another killing on her beach. There's unbearable anxiety hanging over the community."

"I'm in unbearable anxiety as well. Did your résumés bring a response?"

"Overland University asked for an interview. How about you. Any FBI openings in Florida?"

"The Tybourne office wants someone with an accounting background. Lawyers with math skills are scarce as hen's teeth. My only claim is summer work in my dad's office and a minor in accounting."

"Can you fake it? The online outfits give Ph.D.s in ten days."

"Nice try." David chuckled.

"So," Carolyn said, "we'll be a thousand miles apart for awhile longer."

"We'll close the gap this weekend, and I've asked for three days extra." Carolyn didn't answer.

"What's the matter, honey? Do I sense some anxiety not related to the crimes?"

"You do." More silence while David waited. "It's scary," she finally blurted out. "I've never endured this much desire before. It's as if all my nerve endings are wiggling in your direction."

"Friday night. We'll have over an hour together while we wait for your dad's flight."

"Definitely not long enough." She sighed and hung up.

~~~~~~~~~~~

Carl Brockton didn't much care for her conch car, so Carolyn drove to the beach on Friday to get his sedan. He'd asked her to arrange for an oil change and lube job. Little enough to do for her genial, generous father. She'd drive over, get the car lubed, and drive back to Orlando in time to get Timmy from his sitter. He was terribly excited about seeing his grandfather.

Carl's parking slot beneath the building was convenient. It also protected his car's shiny finish from the salt-laden ocean air. Carolyn left her car in front of Byron's unit and took the elevator down. Surprised, she discovered she wasn't alone in the dimly lit cavern below.

Even from the rear she recognized the broad hips of Wanda Wingate.

"Hello," she called. Wanda raised her head, revealing a face flushed with exertion and made even redder because of leaning halfway into a huge freezer chest. Her eyes bulged with surprise then shifted away from Carolyn. She laughed, but it came out more like a snort. A scrub bucket and brush sat on the cement floor next to her feet.

"I didn't mean to startle you," Carolyn added. "It's spooky enough down here without having somebody sneak up behind you."

"That it is. This garage reminds me of the potato cellar on
~~~~~~~~~~~

my dad's farm. Once when I was a little kid I got trapped in there for half a day."

"How awful! What did you do?"

"I cried and screamed and pounded on the door, but nobody heard me. Dad started checking the outbuildings when I didn't show up for supper."

"What a terrible memory! I'd imagine a billion bugs down there in the dark, and I'd still be having nightmares."

"Oh, nothing bothers me," Wanda said. "I sleep like a baby."

Her eyes stared defiantly into Carolyn's, as if daring her to doubt the bold assertion.

The artist in Carolyn leapt to the challenge of drawing Wanda. She'd use oversize rectangles—a large cube for the head and other bulky boxes for the body. She thought of a hippo or a mammoth. No, a Kodiak bear. What about the face? High cheek bones, sort of a Baltic-peasant look. Yet another image flitted across Carolyn's mind. Who else had a similar build and face? Sly Poltron! The two had the same color hair, the same eyes . . .

"Lucky you," Carolyn said. "Sound sleep and a clear conscience. Well, it was nice seeing you. I'm supposed to take Dad's car to be serviced before I meet him at the airport."

"He's is coming back in July? I thought he stayed in Maine until after the leaves drop in the fall. He always raves about the golden glory."

"He's only coming for the party. Dad's nuts about Timmy, and after all the trouble last month, he has even more reason to show up."

"Yes, it's terrible about the boys being kidnapped. What do you think? Will Sly do much time?"

"I think he's learned his lesson. He surely won't try a stunt like that again." That brought a real smile to Wanda's face.

"He surely won't."

"Well, nice seeing you. I'm off to the service bay." Carolyn held up a paperback book. "With something to read."

"I hope it's a juicy murder. Aren't mystery books wonderful?"

"Actually, this one's about the FBI. I figure I'll need it to understand David's job."

"Are you two getting married?" Wanda asked. Carolyn felt her own face flush.

"You don't miss much, do you? Actually we're talking about a wedding. Linda and Mother would like to make all the arrangements, but somehow I think we'll surprise them."

"You'll never get the best of Linda. She's a sharpie."

"You're right."

As she backed out of the stall, Carolyn noticed a piece of black plastic hanging from the pocket of Wanda's shorts. The scene on the beach when she'd met David over a body wrapped in black plastic flashed into her mind.

No! Not Wanda! Not the baby-sitter! Thank God she'd left Timmy in Ovieda, and Martha's two were safe in Iowa. Why in the world would Wanda kill those women? The frozen bodies! Two facts now connected Wanda to the killings.

Carolyn shuddered at the thought of murder in the dark under the building. When the garage doors opened ahead of her she half expected a shot to ring out or the doors to bang down on the car as she drove under them. She gunned the engine and shot up the ramp into the sunlight. Were her suspicions silly?

She used her cell phone to call her sister.

~~~~~~~~~~~

The oil change and lube job took longer than Carolyn had expected, but there was a bit of time before she had to leave for the airport. She drove down into the Tudor Arms garage and parked in her dad's space, planning to use his unit to check her e-mail. Most of her Art Appreciation students should have sent in their answers to her final exam questions by now. She'd print them out and grade the papers while she waited for David and
~~~~~~~~~~~

her dad. Her headlights revealed the freezer with its lid closed, but Wanda was nowhere to be seen.

Inky darkness settled around her when she turned off the car's lights. She groped in her tote bag for the small flashlight she always carried. Using it, she headed for the elevator. Should she go back and park outside? How silly! It could take as much as twenty minutes to print out the exam responses on her dad's antiquated printer.

She shook off the sinister cloak of dread.

But why hadn't the garage lights gone on when she hit the door opener? Power outages on the beach happened often enough. Today, however, there'd been no lightening, no thunder, little wind—and no reason for the electricity to be out. Besides, the motor operating the garage door had worked.

She would stop to see Byron about it before she went to David's unit.

Footsteps sounded behind her, setting her own heart-beats thudding against the walls of her chest.

"Who's there?" Her voice squeaked. She tried to laugh.

Who goes there? Friend or foe?" Easy. Calm down. Nevertheless, she felt inside her bag for a palette knife. It was all she had. The footsteps stopped.

She heard the distant hum of a small motor, but nothing else. Probably an air conditioner. Did the association cool this area? That couldn't be. She reached the elevator door, pushed the lighted up button, and waited. The footsteps came again, heavy and closer, running. She swung her light toward them.

Wanda! With a hypodermic needle!

"You nosey bitch! You're gonna pay." Wanda lunged at her, the needle pointed at her bare shoulder.

Carolyn swung her tote bag at the syringe and jabbed the knife point at Wanda's face. The needle skittered across the cement and Carolyn ran, but Wanda grabbed her by the neck and spun her around. Pain seared Carolyn's throat as incredibly strong fingers pressed into her larynx. She lost her grip on the flashlight. The tote bag slipped from her shoulder and dropped to the floor. She had no time to think about the damaged computer; she kept jabbing at the arm wrapped around her neck.

Damn the stupid knife, flexible when it should have been hard, rounded where it should have had a point. The fingers pressed deeper. Her head was ready to explode. She swung the knife behind her, jabbing for the eyes. Wanda screamed and slammed her to the concrete floor.

Wanda went after the flashlight that had roll under a car, then swung it around in an arc searching the floor.

Carolyn had seconds to escape, but where did safety lie? Running in any direction could end in a bone-jolting crash. Get behind a car. She felt her way around a vehicle, maybe an SUV because of its height and bulk. Could she slither under it and hide? Yes!

Thank God for its oversize tires!

The glowing circle of light worked methodically between the cars. As it advanced toward her she turned pulled herself under the car and behind a wheel. The light passed. Carolyn held her breath a moment before letting herself relax. The footsteps and the light grew fainter. When would it be safe to come out? Where was Linda?

Hadn't she come to check out the freezer?

The footsteps returned, but now a wider circle of light preceded her. This time Carolyn inched closer to the center, away from the sides of the car. The light stopped; the footsteps stopped. Had she made a noise?

When Wanda grabbed her foot, Carolyn twisted and kicked but she was trapped under the SUV. Even as she struggled to pull away, she felt a sharp pain as the needle pierced her thigh.

~~~~~~~~~~
~~~~~~~~~~

Carolyn came around slowly, her mouth as dry as a Styrofoam coffee cup.

Where was she? Tape burned the skin on her face and flattened her lips. She couldn't move her legs, and her hands were firmly fastened behind her. Scratchy carpeting irritated the skin on her shoulders. She could touch walls with her head and with her feet. Musty skirts brushed against her legs. The rank smell of sweat-soaked sneakers assaulted her nose. A thin streak of light shone through the crack under a door. Think. Was she in a unit like hers? Could this be the front-hall closet or the one in the bedroom? The muffled sound of Wanda's voice broke into her fog of silence.

"Of course, dear. I'll take care of myself. Be a sweetie and do the same. I promise you won't be in that hell hole long, No, I won't get caught. They even trusted me with their spoiled brats, and why shouldn't they? We'll be together soon, living as the family we were meant to be. We won't be cheated out of happiness this time." Carolyn held her breath and waited for the next words.

"I shouldn't use the freezer this time? Well then, I could dump her from the dock at Riverside Park. There won't be anybody around after dark, and the deep channel runs close to shore there. I still have the packing box from the new dishwasher, and I'll use the luggage dolly. Yes, I'll be careful, but I still think the freezer works best, with its air-tight seal."

A pause, then the click of the receiver being set back in its cradle.

~~~~~~~~~~~

The knock on Byron's door came at nearly seven o'clock.

"Dad! Hello! What's up?" Reaching out to give his dad a bear hug, Byron locked eyes with the man in the hall behind him. "And David. What brings you back to Sunny Shores so soon?"
~~~~~~~~~~~

"You don't sound happy to see me," David said.

"Cut the crap, Byron," Carl interrupted. "Where is Carolyn?"

"Isn't she with you?" Byron's question made a hole the size of a cannonball in David's stomach. "When I talked to her yesterday," Byron went on, "She said she'd get your car lubed then head for the airport."

"She didn't meet either of our planes, and we haven't heard a word," Carl said. "I've looked in my unit and tried her cell phone."

"She was supposed to meet us two hours ago," David said. "We looked in the garage. The car is in its regular stall, but somebody pulled the lever and cut the electricity. Carolyn's tote bag, computer, and all her stuff is strewn over the floor in front of the elevator."

"If Carolyn didn't bring you," Byron asked, "how did you get here?"

"We waited half an hour," Carl said, "then rented a car. We looked all along 528 on the way over. No accidents or cars by the side of the highway."

"Why didn't you call me?"

"Check your answering machine," Carl said. "Where were you? Out catching waves?" Byron's sheepish grin answered for him.

"It'll be dark soon and hard to see anything," Byron said.

"We know. That's why we didn't wait any longer for her."

"Did you call Linda?" Byron asked.

"Yes," Carl said. "She said Carolyn phoned earlier about Wanda having a freezer in the lower level. Linda is trying to get a judge to sign a search warrant so she can look into it, but she wants us to hunt for Carolyn here before she sends out officers and notifies the highway patrol."

"Police like to wait a few days to look for missing persons," David said, "but when it's your own sister . . . I'd think we know enough to rouse her into action." David grabbed the car keys from the kitchen counter. "We need a plan," he said. Do you have an extra set of Carolyn's keys?"

"Sure do."

"Let's split up the area. You take the streets on the river side of A1A and I'll do those toward the beach. Look for anything unusual." David's voice carried a full load of exasperation.

"Maybe you should check on Wanda first," Carl said. "It's not something I want to think about but . . . "

"Good idea, David said. "We have to find out where that woman is and what she's doing."

"Let's rule out all the possibilities," Carl said. "Take Byron with you. He has my keys to all the units."

~~~~~~~~~~~

The closet door opened. Carolyn twisted her head so she could see her captor.

"So you're awake," Wanda said. "Too bad. I gave you enough to knock out a horse. Some of the stuff must have spilled when you knocked the needle out of my hand." She leaned over to check the tape around Carolyn's wrists and ankles.

"Your rich daddy can't do nothing to help you, and in case you've been praying, the Almighty won't bother to rescue you either." Wanda dragged her across the carpet toward a large empty box.

"You shouldn't have paid so much attention to what I was doing in the garage," she said. "Can't have anybody looking into that freezer, now can we? You think the closet was cramped; just wait until I jam you into it. The motor's running, so it's cooled off nicely."

Carolyn couldn't stop herself from flinching at the idea of being stuffed into a cold, airless chest.

"Aha! That got your attention. Gives you something to think about, now doesn't it. How will it feel to be suffocating ever so slowly as your blood ices up?"
~~~~~~~~~~~

Keep calm, Carolyn told herself. Help is on the way. Concentrate on steady breathing. Think of Timmy. That brought tears to her eyes. No! Don't think of Timmy. Keep calm. Breathe easy. Slow and easy.

The ring of the doorbell made her heart leap.

"Who in the hell . . . " Wanda shoved Carolyn back into the closet and closed the door.

"Who is it?"

"It's Byron."

"I'm getting dressed. Can you wait a minute?"

"No! We need to shut off the power in the building. There's a fire in the main fuse box. Unplug your computer and TV so you don't get a surge. Hurry!"

"Right away. Thanks."

Carolyn began to pound on the wall of the closet with her feet and bang her head against the door. Thank God Byron was looking for her. Her dad must have called. The closet door jerked opened.

~~~~~~~~~~~

Out in the hall, David squelched his desire to strangle Byron. "What kind of cock-and-bull story was that?" he hissed.

"The best I could do. I saw it work once on TV."

"We want inside to look around, but we're still on the wrong side of the door."

"No problem." Byron jingled the huge ring of keys that hung from his belt. "I'm Stan the Man. Ready at your service."

"Cut the crap. It's your sister we're looking for, not some damn sitcom actress on TV." Byron found the key to 707 and used it. While David's blood boiled with impatience, he pushed the door.

"After you, asshole," Byron muttered, and David walked into Wanda's apartment.
~~~~~~~~~~~

"Hello!" he called. "Anybody here?" It took seconds to focus in the dim light. With the sliding glass doors fully opened, wind whipped the gauzy drapes into billowing swirls.

Beyond the curtains Wanda leaned against the balcony railing, holding Carolyn out over a seven story drop.

"You come any closer," she called, "and your precious darling goes splat on the concrete sidewalk." She emphasized her threat with a downward jerk of her head. "Down there."

"What do you want, Wanda." Will Byron have brains enough to go for help? He pushed the door shut behind him, shoving hard against Byron's pressure. Keep her talking, he advised himself. Time is everything.

"My arms are tired. I might drop this spoiled brat any minute." He needed time for Byron to get the fire department with their inflated pads, time to . . . time for what? Think! Why hadn't he paid more attention to this woman?

He knew too damn little about her.

"Let's find a better solution for whatever is wrong," he chose his words carefully. "There's an answer and a happier outcome."

"Don't do that!" she yelled.

"What did I do?" Mustn't panic. Mustn't upset the lady.

"Don't put your hands on your hips. I can't stand any man doing that. Sit down and fold your hands in your lap."

"I was just stretching my back. I think I wrenched it playing with Andrew and Susan." Use the kids names. She may have kindly feelings for them. Play up to the good in her. "Is it all right if I sit on your sofa?" Make her feel the power of place. Wanda said nothing. Sitting on the sofa allowed him to get a few feet closer. Carolyn appeared to be unconscious. Was she still alive? Her feet were dark with pooling blood where the tape had cut off circulation.

"Wouldn't you like to sit down and be comfortable, too?" he asked.

"You look just like my high school principal, the no good son of a bitch!"

"Your principal picked on you?" Wanda's face and arms bore many small cuts. A few of them still bled. She was breathing heavily, her chest heaving, and her voice sounded hoarse. The whites of her eyes glowed in the low light. A dangerously distraught woman.

"Always. Always sneaking around. I know for a fact he had a peek hole into the girls locker room. I heard him tell the gym teacher I had a fat butt, too fat to run. One day I showed him my butt and made him kiss it. Oh, he was a tricky one and you look like him. All pale skin and freckles. You're too scrawny for your own good. You never had to live on potatoes, potatoes, and more potatoes."

Carolyn's head lolled loosely and her arm dangled. Had she fainted or was she drugged?

"You ever do that?" Wanda asked, "peek into the girls dressing room?" He shook his head, afraid of any word that might set her off.

"Well he did."

"Wanda, I can see you're very upset. What can I do to help you?"

"Wanda doesn't take help from anybody, especially not your nosey-copper kind of help. Go away and leave me alone." David kept his face bland. No smiles, which could be construed as superiority, no frowns, which could fuse her rage into action. He kept his voice calm.

"You have something I want very badly. We could make a swap, something you want for something I want."

"I want what everybody else has but I don't ever get. An ordinary life in peace with my son." Wanda's face softened, and her arms curled tighter around Carolyn, drawing the burden inside the railing. David was reminded of a woman cuddling a child. Carolyn extended over Wanda's arms like the Christ figure in the Pieta.

"Tell me about your son. How can we help you have an ordinary life with him?"

"I never got to hold him. Never even seen him all those years, and now you have him locked up." Fresh anger rushed across Wanda's face; she raised Carolyn back over the edge of the railing. "But we talk and he loves me." The impossible connection between Wanda and Sly rocketed through the amazed channels of David's mind.

"Sly Poltron is your son?" Careful. Stay neutral.

"Damn right he is. I traced him here after my father died. Got my mother to move with me to Florida. I've always watched over him like a real mother should."

"I'll get him for you, Wanda. Bring him right here. Let me make a phone call." Wanda rested Carolyn on the railing. When Carolyn opened her eyes, David saw they were black with fright.

"Then what?" Wanda asked. "You'd put him back in jail and me with him. No deal."

"He won't do much time for the stolen goods the officers found. Carolyn's sister is chief of police. If she agrees to the plan, would you take it?" Keep your voice smooth. Don't panic. "And we forget any of this happened." An outright lie. What had Wanda done to Carolyn? "Sly is a fine looking man. You must be very proud of him."

"Quit slicking me up and make your damn call, but I don't move an inch off this balcony." Wanda sat on the porch glider and began to swing. Tears filled Carolyn's eyes as he jabbed at his cell phone. He calculated the steps from the sofa to Wanda's swing. Could he reach the porch before she could stand and throw Carolyn over the railing? Not a good risk to take. He lifted the phone to his ear and waited for Linda to answer.

~~~~~~~~~~~

"She'll be right over with Sly." David said as he pushed the end button.
~~~~~~~~~~~

Wanda's answer was a grunt of disbelief.

"It ain't likely, but I'll wait ten minutes." Time. He was gaining precious time.

"You said you tracked Sly to Florida," David asked. "Was that difficult?" Be careful.

"The home had sealed records, but you can get that stuff if you ask politely. He's a businessman. Don't ever work with his hands. It's a good thing he didn't grow up like I did, dirt poor and scrabbling in the muck of a potato farm. Giving him up was a good thing, maybe."

"You think adoption worked out for the best." Flat words, flat speech.

"I worked with my dad while he lived. Did house and garden work with my mom, too. I always worked all the time. Mom said to get rid of the baby. We couldn't feed another mouth."

"You mentioned high school." Easy. Talk nice. Get friendly.

"Annabel, South Dakota. It's close to the Minnesota border. But you wouldn't know a thing about life up there on the plains." She closed her mouth so hard her lips puffed out. David didn't see anywhere to go with that one. He waited.

"You ask anyone in the building," Wanda said. "If anybody needs help, they always come to Wanda. I'm a good neighbor. The best."

"I'm sure of it. Look at how much you helped my sister with her children. What did you do after high school?"

"After Dad died, I did the field work, all of it. Got good crops, too. Sold them to the chip plant. The spuds had to be just the right size, and no green on them."

"That must have been very difficult for you. Did you have brothers and sisters? Did they do any work."

"Just me. Mom helped out with the planting and harvest. She had to sign the papers. I was too young." Wanda seemed to be relaxing with her memories. She leaned against the backrest and stopped swinging. How can I get her to loosen the tapes around Carolyn's legs. Those feet are painfully swollen.

"She sold out to the neighbor. He wanted more land. Dad would never have done that if he'd lived."

"You wanted to keep working the farm?"

"Land is always there. You don't lose it in a stock market crash or to some damn scheming fraud."

"Has Florida been good to you?" Wanda began to swing again making Carolyn's head loll back and forth. Her eyes had closed again.

Was she drugged? Her body was entirely too limp.

"Can't complain. New motels were going up everywhere when we came. Mom and I found jobs cleaning rooms. I got to be a supervisor, checking the work the others did. It's nice. Living on the beach is nice. Everyone in the building turns to me for help when they need it."

"Wanda, it might be a good idea to loosen the tape around Carolyn's ankles. You can see she needs to get the blood circulating through her feet."

"She cut me up bad. Tried to jab out my eye. I don't know why she did that." David heard the anger building in Wanda's voice.

"Do you still work at the motel, Wanda?" Nice and calm and quiet.

"At the hospital cleaning the OR now. Better pay. Everybody loves me there, too. I do others' work when they need time off. A smile formed on Wanda's face. She looked down at Carolyn, seemed surprised to be holding her, then closed her eyes. Did he dare move toward her?

The door bell rang, and Sly stepped through the door. Wanda's eyes jerked back open. David watched tears form in them, watched her stand. Her arms opened allowing Carolyn to slide to the porch floor.

CHAPTER 16

"Sly honey, things didn't go so well," she said. "They got me trapped." A police officer stood on either side of Sly, with Chief Linda close behind. Wanda looked down at Carolyn. As if realizing her mistake, she scooped her back up and moved closer to the railing.

"This is some party," Wanda said. "Come on in. Never before had so much official company. Who else is in the hall? Where's the mayor?" She laughed. "What happened to Byron?"

So far Sly hadn't opened his mouth, and Linda held her tongue as well. David knew the least thing would set Wanda off and she'd toss Carolyn to her death. Were firemen and their air-filled pads waiting below? Could they catch Carolyn as she fell? David watched Wanda's face darken. Her mood changed as quickly as heavy rains swirl through a storm sewer.

"Don't you have anything to say, like 'Hello Mom', or 'can I help you?'" Wanda snarled. "Something nice after all I've done for you."

"You're the one that put me in jail. You made the ricin yourself and got me to do your dirty work on the old man. Stealing a TV and bringing it to me was a dumb idea. Very dumb. It's ruined my business."

Sly managed to look both superior and angry at the same time. David's eyes shifted from Sly to Wanda and back. Quite possibly Sly really was her biological son. Same thick upper body and round face, same straight mouths with thin lips. Both had fine hair, but judging from the dark roots, Wanda bleached hers.

"Mr. Worthan didn't bring charges. It's not my fault they locked you up."

"Anybody who pokes around in a pawn shop long enough will find something that shouldn't be there. Without that damn TV, these cops didn't have a reason to search my store."

Was there anything in Sly's statements that David could use to save Carolyn? He watched every movement Wanda made, trying to assess her emotions. Did that flicker in the muscle under her jaw mean impatience or anger? Or both?

"I got Mazie, Miriam, and Agnes Wellington to sign their deeds over to you," Wanda said. "Be properly grateful. That's maybe nine hundred thousand dollars I delivered to you. Nearly a million. More money than I ever had or ever will." Wanda continued to hold Carolyn in her arms as she lurched closer to the railing. David poised to make a dash. He could grab for Carolyn's legs.

"It wasn't my idea to get rid of the old ladies," Sly said. Wanda gasped and Sly's face flushed. He'd probably blurted out the truth without thinking.

"I didn't mean . . . " Sly said. He looked at David, shrugged, and faced Wanda. "You just wanted a plot for your goddamn mystery book. Needed bodies, needed a killer. Wanted to be famous so the people back in the Dakotas would see your book and be impressed."

"That's not true and you know it. Those women came around every day telling me their troubles. Couldn't make it, didn't have enough to buy food. Didn't I feed them breakfast and lunch whenever I could?"

"Your fucking good deeds didn't need to end in three murders. They ate your grub one time too many."

"You grew the stuff."

"Hell, castor beans are all over my place. I never used it to kill anybody." Wanda raised Carolyn over the edge of the railing with effort. She seemed tired, drained of her enormous strength, but she made one last try at Sly.

"Call me Mother," she said. "Just once I want to hear you say it. Act like you're grateful. I can't undo what happened to you the past twenty-seven years, but you can damn well learn decent manners now."

"I'm sure your son loves you, Wanda," David interrupted. "Why don't you let us take Carolyn, and we'll all leave. You and Sly can work things out together." Wanda shook her head and looked over the edge of the balcony.

"Seven floors down," she said. "I'm giving your girlfriend the thrill of her life. Too bad she's not awake to enjoy the trip." She swung Carolyn back, preparing to throw her over the railing. David tore across the room, but it felt as if he were swimming in crude oil. He couldn't possibly reach the porch in time.

"You can have her," Wanda shrieked, "every stinking piece of her that's left."

The rumble came first, then a sharp crack as the railing bulged outward. Loosened from its wall supports, it pulled Wanda farther outward. She dropped Carolyn onto the porch floor to save herself. Her hands gripped the posts, but the very metal bars she clung to in desperation pulled her away from what little safety existed. The railing gave way and the floor itself began to break off.

As Wanda tumbled out into space, David grabbed Carolyn and dragged her into the room. Linda and the policemen rushed to help him. They pulled Carolyn to safety, but the entire platform broke away. Wanda's screams grew fainter, then ceased.

Sly bolted into the hall. The stunned officers got themselves together and raced after him. Linda grabbed her cell phone to call the EMT's.

The officers tackled Sly before he reached the elevator and threw him face down on the carpet while they cuffed his wrists behind him.

"Get that damn book," he yelled. "She wrote it all down. I didn't kill a one of them women. I'm telling the truth. Get the book."

~~~~~~~~~~~

Was there any hope for Wanda? An awning that would break her fall? Bushes at the edge of the walk? Seven floors, fifty -six feet. He'd seen it once—a suicide lying on the sidewalk in front of a downtown Kansas City hotel—he didn't want ever to see it again. But no: the heavy concrete porch floor must have landed on top of Wanda, crushing whatever chance she'd had to survive the fall.

~~~~~~~~~~~

Minutes after the accident an EMT knelt in front of Carolyn, cutting through the tape around her ankles while David freed her wrists. When they'd finally removed the tape plastered across her mouth, David took her in his arms.

"I'll talk non-stop," she mumbled through swollen lips. "Never shut up. I can't get over having my mouth taped. You can't imagine, I felt like a wooden doll with a mass of emotions stuffed inside and no way to express them. My entire body burns with the tension."

"How are your feet? They must hurt like hell. Let me rub them."

"No you don't, my friend," the EMT said. "They need

elevation and ice. I'll give her something for the pain. Nothing more. Especially no rubbing!" Carolyn shook her head.

"Wanda had something in a syringe. You'd better not add another medication to whatever she jabbed into me."

"Good thinking." The EMT nodded.

"David, could you get me a drink? Water, tea, anything."

"Nothing but water until we find out what she gave you," the EMT said.

Carolyn held her hand out toward him. "What am I thinking of? I should kiss you for getting me loose, but please let me introduce myself. I'm Carolyn Brockton, your chief's sister."

"Officer Teddy Hopkins. Glad to help." His grin would spread a glow into the darkest corner of any cave.

"What's going on down below?" she asked. "Was anybody else hurt?"

"I don't think so. There wasn't a thing we could do for her so the chief sent me up here. Do you know where that syringe is?" Carolyn shook her head.

"Maybe it's in her pocket. She said she'd given me enough to knock out a horse."

"I'll look around in here then go check her body. They should have the rubble off her by now." As soon as he left David wrapped his arms around Carolyn; she leaned her head against his chest.

"You're not the only one going through emotional hell today," he said.

"You came in like an answer to my prayers. Wanda said God wouldn't help, but He must have sent you."

"Carl and I were worried when you didn't show up. We looked on both sides of the highway all the way back to the beach. Your car was here, and your dad's sat in the garage. Your stuff was spilled over the floor in front of the elevator."

"I hoped somebody would notice that. Wanda was furious when I dumped it out, but she didn't take time to pick it up."

"Your dad sent us here to check."

"I nearly forgot—you need to examine the freezer in the basement for traces of the murdered women."

"What's that all about?"

"The freezer. That's how this all started. I came upon Wanda cleaning it out before I took the car for servicing."

EPILOGUE

Sunday morning, July 4th, the following year...

Luminescent waves washed ashore in the everlasting pulse of life.

"Mother, did you pray that David and I would get married?" Carolyn asked.

"I prayed that you'd be happy, and I planned for your wedding. There's a difference." Monica's red hair gleamed in the early morning light, and her eyes danced with happiness. "It's not true that only good girls get their prayers answered."

"You and Linda got exactly what you wanted, and we love it," David said. He reached across Timmy to touch the new gold band on Carolyn's finger. "The artist and the agent, united as one. It was a lovely wedding. Thank you, Mother." Linda stood and raised her glass of orange juice.

"The new children's center is a wonderful place," Monica said.

"I've been wanting a good after-school facility for years," Linda said. "Agnes Wellington drew love like a magnet, so those who knew her donated more-than-enough money to build it."

"By the way," Linda added, "I hear Allison dropped her suit to get Timmy back."

"That she did," Carolyn said, "but not before the court-appointed guardian ad litem reported that her apartment was filthy and unfit for a child to live in." That drew a chuckle from David.

"That report plus the photographs of Allison entering her apartment near midnight with three different men," David said. "She could not go to court and face that powerful information. Even with her high class rank, if the pictures were entered into court records, she would never get a good job in law."

"The sun will be up soon. Look at the sky," Monica pointed out. "Carolyn, Linda, and Byron should do the honors. Agnes was their favorite." The group grew solemn as they plodded across the soft gray sand to the shoreline. The three siblings waded out into the surf. They opened the box at the very moment the sun hovered round and huge and brilliant above the line separating ocean from sky.

"May the goodness and kindness of Agnes Edna Wellington spread around the world," Carolyn said, sprinkling the remains over the shimmering waters.

David watched the film of ashes disappear into the retreating surf. The sheer beauty of the dawn's aurora made him want to fall on his knees in gratitude, but he took the empty box from Carolyn and carefully replaced the lid.

"Come on," he said. "It's time to head for Paradise Island."

As they walked away from the shore, Paulette ran up to them. "Don't worry, Aunt Carolyn. I will take good care of your cats. "

Carolyn gave her niece a hug. "I am very sure you will be the best cat-sitter ever."

At those words, Paulette's smiling face clouded over. She said, "But mom says they cannot sleep in my bed."

With one more hug for Paulette, Carolyn left for her honeymoon with David, who carried his newly adopted son Timmy.

Don't Miss These Other Great Titles By Evelyn Wolph Kruger

(Available through Amazon, Barnes & Noble and Old Line Publishing)

Revolutionary Rose: Boston Tea to Boston Free

Redeeming Grace

Stalking Sadie

CPSIA information can be obtained at www.ICGtesting.com
Printed in the USA
LVOW04s1117131015

458059LV00018B/233/P